Rupa Bajwa was born in 1976 in Amritsar, India. She is still grappling with the notion of a fixed address. This is her second novel. She is currently working on her third novel.

Praise for *Tell Me a Story*

'Bajwa has a way with language. She writes with ease and impeccable fluency, her character descriptions flawless as she eases the reader into the lives of various protagonists …'

Dawn

'Her restrained telling is reminiscent of Kamala Markandaya's work.'

Hindustan Times

'Bajwa tells her story simply and directly. The pace is absorbing and the environment realistic.'

The Statesman

'Rupa's strengths as a novelist lie in her ability to take an ordinary character and spin a captivating story out of the parenthesis of everyday routine.'

Elle

'Rupa Bajwa writes in an unpretentious, small-town English perfectly suited to her unpretentious, small-town heroine.'

The Hindu

'… a superb use of the telling detail.'

Deccan Herald

'… Bajwa's low-key approach to story-telling is so refreshing.'

DNA

'Bajwa's story is sincere and satisfying …'

Time Out

Also by Rupa Bajwa

The Sari Shop (2004)

Tell Me a Story

Rupa Bajwa

PICADOR INDIA

First published in the Indian subcontinent 2013 by Picador
an imprint of Pan Macmillan, a division of Macmillan Publishers Limited
Pan Macmillan, 20 New Wharf Road, London N1 9RR
Basingstoke and Oxford
Associated companies throughout the world
www.panmacmillan.com

ISBN 978-1-447-21774-9

1 3 5 7 9 8 6 4 2

Typeset in Sabon Lt Std 10/13 by Jojy Philip, New Delhi 110015
Printed and bound in India by Replika Press Pvt. Ltd.

For my parents:
Rajwant Bajwa
and
Swarn Singh Bajwa
who have always, ever since I can remember,
sat in dark rooms with me, waiting patiently
till I was ready to step out into the light

'Only he is an emancipated thinker who is not afraid to write foolish things.'

– Anton Chekhov

I

One

The sky was a dark grey. Fat raindrops lashed the swollen wood of the kitchen window and splattered their way into the kitchen, making dark circles on the slightly dusty floor.

Rani sprinted to the kitchen window to close it. She reached through the bars and pulled at the heavy, swinging window, her solitary silver bangle getting caught in the bars.

Raindrops trembled on her chipped nail polish.

Rani pursed her lips in concentration and pulled again. The wood was rough under the skin of her fingertips. She made a final effort with both her hands and shot the bolt quickly, before the window could creak and swing out happily again.

Rani absently shook her hands dry. She was worried. The whole house was giving way under the onslaught of the monsoon this time. The walls were damp, a corner of the roof leaked, the doors and windows were swollen and had vertical, squiggly cracks in them. It had been bad during the last monsoon but the house had held out. This year, it was visibly giving way. Rani knew they could not afford the repairs that the roof would need, let alone the cost of replacing doors and windows.

Then her mind wandered back to her nail polish. She would remove it today and paint her nails afresh with two coats, a nice pale pink instead of her regular maroon, a shade of pink she had seen Aishwarya Rai wear in an advertisement for a shampoo recently.

✧ ✧ ✧

Rani turned back to the ancient stove on the floor and, squatting, added chopped potatoes to the subzi she was making. Neelam walked into the kitchen, dragging Bittu by the ear. 'Eight years old and can't be trusted to take a bath on his own,' she was shouting.

Rani looked up. 'What happened *now*?'

'Do you know what this wretched fellow was doing?'

'What?'

'There is no money in the house and this prince had put the whole bar of soap into a bucket full of water to make *soap bubbles*. He says he *likes the feel* of soap bubbles!' She pulled at Bittu's ear and he yelled.

Rani looked at him and giggled. His thin little arms were soapy up to the elbows. He grinned back at her, rubbing his red ear.

'Ma, you are a Hitler lady.'

Neelam looked teary. 'That bar of soap cost twelve rupees.'

Rani tried to sober up. 'Don't worry, Bhabhi. What is done is done.'

'You be quiet, Rani. You encourage him in all his nonsense. Yesterday, he broke the only glass in the house. All we have left are the steel tumblers now.' Neelam's delicate nostrils quivered and her face looked pinched.

She had been worried lately too.

Rani motioned to Bittu to not speak. Once Neelam got worked up, it was best to keep quiet. Rani covered the simmering kadhai and pulled Bittu down to the solitary tap in the kitchen. She washed his arms free of the soapy coating and dried them with her chunni. Neelam, after banging various utensils and jars, finally started to knead dough, still perturbed. 'Why are you spoiling your chunni? It is almost time for you to go to work.'

'What does it matter?' Rani said. 'It is so wet outside. Even with an umbrella, I'll get drenched. A little damp spot on the chunni won't matter.'

'Are you going to borrow an umbrella from next door again?' Neelam asked disapprovingly.

'What to do?' Rani said gloomily. 'I have been trying to save up for one for the last three months. The cheapest one is for 120 rupees. I bargained it down to a hundred. But where is the hundred at the end of the month?'

The two women were silent for a while. Bittu stared at each of them in turn.

'Sugar has gone up even more this month,' Neelam said.

There was a still silence in the small kitchen for a while, except for the sound of Rani stirring the thin potato gravy with a long-handled spoon, the slapping of Neelam's hands against the damp lump of dough and the jingling of her glass bangles.

Then Bittu's voice piped up, 'I can make an umbrella for you,' he offered, looking at Rani. 'Maybe with a stick and a plastic sheet ...'

'You be quiet,' Neelam snapped at him. 'You don't do a scrap of schoolwork. Not a single word of English do you know. All those children at big convent schools can chatter in English at your age, and look at you. Umbrella indeed!'

Bittu looked confused for a moment then recovered his poise. 'I am the best at adding and subtracting in my class,' he boasted.

'Go and get dressed for school,' Neelam said shortly. Bittu left, dragging his feet. Rani fished out a piece of potato with a spoon and broke it with her fingers to check if it was done. Satisfied, she turned the gas off and got up. She knew from the look on Neelam's face that she had gone into one of her moody silences.

✧ ✧ ✧

Dheeraj Kumar finished his morning prayers in the small corner above which he hung pictures of various Hindu deities and a print of Guru Nanak's portrait. On a rough, protruding shelf rested a small statue of the Buddha, a Sai Baba postcard and a brass holder for incense and dhoop.

The rain made his joints hurt. He draped his old cotton shawl around his shoulders and picked up his copy of *Dainik Bhaskar*, hoping to find a corner of the house where he could read undisturbed.

He had no such luck. The tiny verandah where he usually sat was being sprayed wet with the rain. In the hall, his son Mahesh stood, sullenly brushing his teeth, looking out of the window at the puddles forming in the street outside. 'No work today?' Dheeraj asked, with a show of geniality. Mahesh managed to mumble through his meagre toothpaste foam. 'Later, when the rain stops. I'll do the later shift.' Neelam insisted that everyone use only a tiny blob of toothpaste on their brushes. It was enough, she said, and a tube of toothpaste could last four times longer that way.

Dheeraj nodded and made his way towards the corner of the dim room which was lit by a single tube light. He switched it on even though he knew Neelam frowned upon the use of lights during daytime. He just hoped his daughter-in-law wouldn't notice, and if she did, wouldn't comment on it. He sat huddled under the tube light, reading about honour killings, chain snatching and inflation on the front page of *Dainik Bhaskar*.

✧ ✧ ✧

The rain continued to pour down with fury. The house was small, and very old. Rani's grandfather had bought it after three decades of saving – a tiny structure tucked away in the endless warren of houses and streets in the old city.

The house was shaped like an L. Rani and Bittu lived and slept in the longer leg of the L, which had been grandly christened 'the hall' by the two, even if it was stacked with battered tin trunks, rusty, unused utensils, an old brown attaché case of Dheeraj's, and various other odds and ends. On the top of one tin trunk sat a small television set, their proudest possession.

Bittu did his homework here, sitting cross-legged on a chatai, and Rani had a small steel almirah in which she kept her clothes. At night they slept there, rolling out their mattresses and lying side by side. Before sleeping, Bittu would sometimes turn over on his stomach, push his pillow away, pull down the bedcover and with crayons and sketch pens that he kept stashed in a red box nearby, he would draw things on the mattress. Mostly he drew monkeys and bicycles. Occasionally he would write a word or two. His mother had stopped him, scolded him and even slapped him once but since he could see no actual harm in it, Bittu continued. He'd wait till the lights were out and would draw by the light of the street lamp outside. Rani never bothered to stop him. Sometimes at bedtime Rani and Bittu would talk idly. Occasionally, Bittu would clamour for stories. Rani's stories were energetic and highly imaginative, but she never managed to finish them. They started with high drama but petered off to nothing. This always left Rani feeling confused and a little baffled.

The smaller arm of the L was curtained off by a bed sheet. Dheeraj lived in this space. It was the neatest, tidiest part of the whole house. Here he prayed, slept on his old charpai and kept all his belongings in a pre-Partition black trunk.

A tiny kitchen and a very, very small room had managed to fit themselves off the hall. Mahesh and Neelam slept in this room. It could accommodate only a small double bed that Neelam's parents had given her at their wedding, despite Dheeraj's protests. He was against dowry. But Neelam's parents did not pay much attention to him. People hardly ever did.

Bittu refused to sleep in his parents' room. To him, the room seemed too small and he was secretly sure that the spirit of Jaggu, their dead school watchman, lurked under the bed. A classmate of his had told him that old Jaggu visited the homes of all the boys who had ever made fun of him. Though Bittu did not remember doing that, why take risks, he thought. Bittu preferred the hall, Rani's bedtime stories and the freedom from the watchful maternal eye.

A cubicle-sized lavatory and a bathroom were tucked away behind these rooms, with only rusty ventilators high up in the walls serving for light.

There was a courtyard in the front, with just enough space in it for a neem tree, a corner for Mahesh's bicycle, with a little patch left for a charpai in the winter months. Every monsoon, when the earth of the courtyard became wet and slippery, they debated whether to have it cemented over or not.

But the monsoon would pass. And they would forget.

✧ ✧ ✧

Rani looked at herself in the specked mirror in the green plastic frame hanging on the wall. She unplaited her hair and ran a comb through it, then plaited it again neatly. Her face looked back at her. She had plain, ordinary features and straight, dark brown hair. Only her large eyes could, at a stretch, be considered beautiful but Rani wasn't too sure about that either.

Rani adjusted her chunni, picked up a plastic bag, balanced it flat on the top of her head and went out onto the verandah. There was a strong wind outside as well as the rain, and it blew spray on her face. Rani ran down the two crumbling stone steps from the verandah and ran across the slushy courtyard to the boundary wall.

'Seema,' she screamed over the noise of the rain. Her nostrils sucked up the smell of the wet, mossy wall. She waited a moment. A slight girl with a hooked nose poked her head out the front door next door, and flashed a brilliant smile at Rani.

Seema was Rani's friend as well as her next-door neighbour. Hers was a large joint family. There was a grandmother, brothers, sisters-in-law, their offsprings and a constant stream of visiting relatives and friends who always seemed to bring their whole brood along. Since Rani got along well with Seema and visited her often, Bittu took every opportunity to accompany her and participate in the perpetual chaos next door. He was special friends with Seema's nephew, Karan, who was exactly Bittu's age.

'What?' Seema shouted back.

'Umbrella,' Rani bellowed, raindrops dripping onto her shoulders from the edges of the plastic bag she held over her head. Seema disappeared and was back soon with an ugly red-and-black umbrella. She ran lightly towards the wall over which she handed it to Rani. The girls grinned at each other, feeling exhilarated by the rain. Rani snatched the umbrella and then both ran back to their respective front doors, giggling hysterically in the downpour. It seemed a happy morning.

✧ ✧ ✧

When she went back indoors, Bittu was in his school uniform – light blue shirt and navy blue pants – with the unnaturally tidy, combed hair of early-morning schoolboys. He looked at the umbrella in her hand a little derisively. 'If nobody carried umbrellas,' he said musingly, 'everyone would be allowed to get wet. It would be much nicer.'

'Do you know what pneumonia is?' Rani asked him.

'Not really.'

'Then ask your teacher today, and run off now. I have to get dressed and leave.'

'Sometimes you make no sense,' Bittu said, hoisting his school bag over his shoulder. He waved at her, rushed to touch his grandfather's feet and finally left for school.

Rani began to check her purse for her money, change for the tempo and the Crocin Pain Relief tablets that she always carried with her. Dheeraj looked up from his newspaper and gazed at his daughter thoughtfully. 'You know, I still think you should have continued with school. For whatever it was worth. Even though I know you disliked it, had problems. You could have studied a little more. You were close to your ninth-standard exams. Another year and you would have been at least tenth pass. Maybe,' he said hesitantly, 'you could have even ...'

Rani looked up at him enquiringly. 'I mean,' he said, his voice a little awkward now, 'you could have even become a schoolteacher.'

There was a pause.

'But I like my work. I am happy, Papaji,' Rani replied. They had talked about this so many times yet Dheeraj always brought it up as if it had occurred to him for the first time. It had almost become a daily morning ritual.

'You are happy. Now,' he said. 'But I am not sure how it will be later.'

'We'll see then,' Rani said lightly. 'Later.'

'What can you do later? You'll be stuck forever. I should have insisted then. Now it is too late.'

Rani didn't answer.

'It is often too late,' Dheeraj said, looking into the distance.

Then he returned to his *Dainik Bhaskar*.

Rani said her goodbyes and rushed off, not noticing Mahesh, who stood still in the verandah now, not minding the spray.

He looked at his sister's retreating back resentfully as she skipped and jumped her way over the puddles. What was the reason for her pointless joy?

And then he immediately felt guilty.

Two

When Rani reached Eve's Beauty Parlour for Ladies, where she worked, her Bata chappals were caked with mud. She took them off outside and slipped on the pretty mauve regulation slippers that all the girls who worked there wore inside. She studied them for a while, wishing that they were blue ones with tiny sunflowers on them, the kind she had seen in a shop window the other day. There were other open, dripping umbrellas parked outside the door. Rani parked hers with them and stepped in. Asha, the woman who owned and ran the parlour, wasn't around. Her living quarters were behind the parlour. She often unlocked the front door in the mornings to let the girls in and then went off to finish chores in the house while the girls readied themselves and the parlour for customers.

The main door of Eve's Beauty Parlour opened into a small, well-lit cheerful reception area that was discreetly screened off from the main room by a Chinese lacquered screen. It contained a reception desk, two chairs upholstered in red velvet and a few posters of French models posing for international beauty products. Rani always felt flummoxed by the strange women in these posters. Their looks, their skinniness, their impractical make-up and clothes – none of it made sense to her.

Secretly, Rani felt they could not have much common sense.

Past the screen were mirror-lined walls and expensive chairs facing them, display racks that held beauty products, a sink for shampoos and various cabinets and drawers that held beautyconnected paraphernalia. At one end of the room were two massage tables for facials, curtained off from each other by a blue-and-yellow floral-patterned cloth. The light over these tables could be dimmed. Asha had got these lights specially installed. She had seen them in one of the magazines she read and knew that swanky parlours in Delhi and Bombay used them too. She had considered the matter carefully and then had written to order them as soon as she could afford them. She was so protective of them that she would not let any of the girls touch the regulator, rushing herself to the switchboard every time the lights needed to be dimmed.

A door led to a small bathroom. A notice on the door said, 'Smile, it makes you beautiful'. There was also a curtained-off alcove where the girls had a couple of chairs to sit on during lunch, a cupboard to store their things in and a small red stove they could use to make tea.

The parlour was not very large but Asha had done her best to make good use of the space, agonizing over each detail.

✧ ✧ ✧

Mahesh sneaked a look at the old clock that had been hanging on the dingy wall of the factory ever since he could remember. There was still an hour to go before his shift ended. He had been working the power loom for more than six hours and the shawl was still not complete. The best factories in Amritsar paid you monthly salaries, but he had only heard of them. Others paid daily wages. His boss, Charan Das, did too.

By the time he was done, it had stopped raining but the evening was hot, unbearably humid. His body was drenched in sweat, his temples ached and his hair stuck to his scalp. He said goodbye to the other workers and wheeled his bicycle out into the road, glad to be free of the oppressiveness of the factory, its lack of ventilation and the constant noise.

Mahesh stood there with his cycle for a few minutes, savouring a few moments of peace. A few steps away from his feet, he saw flies swarming over a piece of rotting mango that a fruit seller had discarded there.

Some of the flies barely moved, desperately clinging to the sweetness.

Mahesh bought a beedi from a cigarette stall nearby. On some days he'd buy a cigarette, but it always made him feel guilty. After all, there was tobacco in both and a cigarette was more expensive. He lit the beedi and smoked it standing by his bicycle.

The flies on the mango remained in place. Workers from the factory – shadowy, tired figures – were leaving the building and disappearing down different streets, some to gather at favourite drinking spots, others to their homes, till they returned the next day. When they would be back in the hot confines of the factory, working the power looms to produce beautiful shawls that were exported to countries that they did not even know the names of.

Mahesh sighed. Thanks to his father and the strange mix of education and illiteracy in their home, he knew the names of some of the countries.

He knew how much the shawls produced in this poky corner of Amritsar were sold for.

And he knew how much he and his co-workers got paid.

The usual constant cold anger throbbed in his head.

He finished his beedi, threw it on the ground and instead of stubbing it, stood still, watching it till it died.

His limbs stiff and aching, he mounted his cycle and began to pedal his way homewards. Most of the streetlights on the road did not work. The few that did threw beautiful reflections in the puddles on the rained-on road, till Mahesh rode his bicycle bumpily through the puddles, stirring up the mud. Then the twinkling water vanished and a murky mess sent up droplets of mud that splattered Mahesh's feet and his pants.

✧ ✧ ✧

The day had gone much easier for Rani. The rain, instead of depressing, seemed to have lifted the spirits of all the girls.

Rani had gone to the cupboard that held their stuff, with one small shelf allotted to each of them. She put away her purse and took out the red-and-white checked apron that all of them wore over their street clothes during work hours. She slipped it on over her clothes.

Dolly, who considered herself the prettiest of them all with her fair skin and sharp nose, stood in front of one of the mirror-lined walls, examining the shape of her eyebrows critically. 'You didn't do these too well,' she remarked to Kavita.

Kavita looked indignant. 'Oh, is it? Is Madam a customer that she is complaining? Madam is not pleased? Madam wants a refund? I stayed back just to do them. Ungrateful cat! Your eyebrows have a basically strange shape. Not my fault. Very, very strange shape.'

Dolly looked offended for a fleeting moment then laughed. 'Really?' she said.

'Yes, really. Madam, if you are not pleased, do them yourselves in future.''Dolly, Kavita!' said Navpreet sternly, 'Quiet! The fresh towels still need to be folded. One of you do that right now and the other get down to boiling the combs and brushes. I will make tea today.'

Navpreet, though called 'one of the girls', was actually a heavyset woman in her late thirties, a widow who had to fend for herself. She considered herself in charge in Asha's absence, something that all the other girls resented.

'Oh, the Prime Minister of India has spoken,' Kavita muttered under her breath. Dolly sniggered. The two wandered off to their tasks. Navpreet busied herself at the little stove in the alcove, measuring water for tea, and Rani was left alone with Shama and Mani.

✧ ✧ ✧

'Rain is so romantic,' Shama said with a sigh, looking out of the glass window at the trees outside, twirling the end of her tasselled chunni around her fingers dreamily. She was addicted to films that were love stories.

Mani shook her head at Shama in exasperation. She had never been able to figure this silly girl out. She answered shortly, 'Rain makes puddles. Messy. And power cuts.'

Rani listened to them absently, scrubbing her hands with Dettol soap, as Asha had instructed all of them to do everyday before commencing work.

Asha came in just as the first customer walked in, and the buzz that would last for the rest of the day began. The girls suddenly looked less silly, Asha's usually vague face took on a competent expression, drawers began to open and shut. Efficiency crackled in the air. The customer, a harried-looking woman, said breathlessly, 'Eyebrows and upper lip, also bleach, and I have to go and prepare for a lunch party, so quickly.'

Asha gave her a comforting smile, as if she had never been harried and rushed herself ever and said soothingly, 'Sit, sit. Relax. One minute only. Rani, bleach. Navpreet, eyebrows.' Then, with another smile, 'There is enough time. Hair colour? Blow-dry?'

The woman looked uncertain then settled into a chair while the girls hovered over her. More customers began to drift in.

By afternoon Rani had done two facials, one pedicure, and had shaped about six pairs of eyebrows. She rather enjoyed eyebrows. She was about to settle down and have lunch from her steel tiffin box when Kavita came to her and said in a sibilant whisper, 'Phone call for you.'

Rani was surprised. Nobody was supposed to call them at the beauty parlour unless it was an emergency. She felt a stab of panic in her heart and got up quickly, making her way to the tiny front room. She picked up the phone, staring at the impossibly beautiful French models on the silly posters that Asha had so painstakingly bought on a trip to New Delhi.

'Hello?' Rani said breathlessly into the receiver.

'Rani Bua?' Bittu's voice said.

Rani's heart sank.

'Bittu? What happened? Are you okay? Where are you?'

'At Karan's house,' he replied.

'What are you doing there? Is everything alright?' Rani could feel her heartbeat.

'School is over,' he replied.

'Yes, but what … why are you calling?'

'To see if you are there.'

'Where?'

'Where you said to call if it was an emergency.'

'But what is the matter?'

'Nothing. Just checking to see if you are there on this number. So, what are you doing?' he asked conversationally.

Rani let out a breath she didn't realize she had been holding.

'You little monkey! How did you get this number?' Rani asked, trying to speak in a controlled voice.

'Papaji's diary. I copied it in my maths book. You know, for emergencies, as you said.'

'Where is Karan's mother?' Rani asked sternly.

'Temple,' Bittu answered. 'She had a thali with her. Four fat, sweet laddoos in it. All to offer to God. None for us.'

'Who is at Karan's home?' Rani asked tersely.

'His grandmother. Beeji. She is sleeping. You know, Rani Bua,' Bittu continued leisurely, 'she has false teeth. A whole set. I just saw it. In a glass. Did you know that people could have extra sets?'

Rani looked around to check if Asha was around.

'Bittu, what you need is a tight slap that will knock all your teeth out. Then you can also have an extra set. I'll tell Neelam Bhabhi that you called here. And you shouldn't use people's telephones without asking. Rest I'll tell you when I get home. Junglee!'

With that, she hung up and went back to her lunch, slightly shaken. Asha was strict about the phone calls rules.

'Who was it?' Dolly asked.

Rani didn't answer. She was famished by now and just wanted to eat.

'Ooh. Boyfriend?' Dolly said in delight.

Navpreet barked at her from the other end of the room, 'Dolly, where *is* the jar of fruit face pack?'

Dolly scuttled away. Rani opened her box to find that the aloo subzi had leaked and the rotis were soggy. Kavita, who came in to change her face bleach-splattered apron, said, 'What a feast!'

Rani said sarcastically, 'And I suppose you've got tandoori chicken for lunch?'

'No, no, I am going to Mohan's International for lunch. The best five-star hotel in Amritsar.'

Mani, coming in to comb her unruly hair, overheard. 'Those people are mad,' she said blandly. 'These five-star people. I have heard about them. Seventy rupees for a cup of tea.' In her crisp voice, she added, 'No common sense.'

Kavita looked shocked. 'That much?'

'That is nothing. In bigger cities they are worse,' Mani said informatively.

'Faulty wiring in their brains then,' Kavita said. 'No, Rani? Imagine that!'

Forgetting all about the apron she had come to change, Kavita settled down and asked Mani, 'How much for other things?'

'I am not a waiter. How do I know? I've just heard it is like that.'

'You know, even here in Amritsar, there is this hotel which charges 200 rupees for a plate of Chinese fried rice,' Kavita began, and then Navpreet yelled for her too. 'Kavita, turn the geyser on. And get the pedicure tub.'

Kavita sighed and left, without changing her apron. She reappeared again in half a minute. 'Uff,' she said, quickly taking her apron off and pulling on another. 'I must have killed a cow or something in my last birth. No wonder I have a tough life.' She disappeared again.

Mani, who had now got her hair in a neat, tight plait, said, 'It is not always cows,' and left.

✧ ✧ ✧

Rani sighed when she was finally alone in the alcove and gratefully ate her soggy rotis, enjoying the first minutes of peace she had got since the day had begun. She wondered how many more eyebrows and faces and hairdos the day held. Facials could get tiring. The wedding season was more fun, when people came in more for make-up and to get their hands decorated with mehndi patterns. Rani finished her lunch and stretched. There were three more hours of work, and then she would go home, make herself a hot cup of tea and watch a film on Zee Cinema.

Rani thought back to what her father had said that morning. She knew he did not think much of either the beauty parlour or of Zee Cinema. In fact, he seemed slightly perplexed by both. She idly wondered if her life would have been much different if she had continued with school. What a school, she thought! More a morgue!

Rani had hated her school – the prison-like iron gates, the dilapidated building, their grim little classroom with the walls whitewashed a dirty pistachio green, the creaking fan that seldom worked, leaving the girls and the teacher sweltering and perspiring through most of the summer. The classroom smelt of sweat, chalk and cheap talcum powder. Their class teacher, Mrs Madhu Chauhan, addressed as Madhu Madam by the girls, was a bleak-looking woman with flared nostrils and sad eyes. She taught them all the subjects in a droning, depressing voice.

Rani had managed to plod her way mechanically to Class Nine. She got along fairly well with her classmates, though she had no special friend. She had a flair for telling stories, which made her popular with the other girls, most of whom attended the Government School for Girls in a spirit of resignation and boredom.

One morning, Madhu Madam entered the classroom with a sheaf of corrected papers of a mathematics class test and a grim expression on her face. The girls straightened in their seats. Madhu Madam took her seat and sighed.

'These are your maths test results. You have all done very, very badly. The highest marks are Meenu's – 60 out of 100,' here everyone turned to look at Meenu, who looked self-conciously at the wall. 'But your class should be applauded for having a student who has the lowest marks in maths than I have ever seen.'

There was a dramatic pause.

'15 out of 100! Shocking! Rani, stand up.'

Rani stood up, aware of the gaze of all the girls on her.

'Have you got brains or straw in your head? You will never get anywhere in life, I am sure of that. Now keep standing till recess.'

Then Madhu Madam commenced teaching, giving them a hard time by asking questions and being sarcastic.

By the time the bell was rung by recess, and the teacher left the room, Rani's feet were aching. She sat down in relief and put her head on the desk.

The girls either went out to the grounds with their tiffin boxes or stayed in class and ate. Since it was drizzling outside, today they remained in. One of the girls called out to her, 'Don't worry about that witch, Rani. I have heard that her husband just left her for another woman. I don't blame him.'

The girls laughed and giggled and then one turned to Rani and said, 'She has given me a headache today. What about telling us a story?'

Rani felt too tired to make up one but more girls clustered around her, clamouring for a story. So Rani, in her usual random way, began. It turned out to be a particularly enthralling one, taking Rani and the girls away from the mundane reality of the classroom to a world of very small creatures who lived right under the surface of the earth. They lived so deep inside that even if humans dug deep wells, they could not reach them. Rani became animated as she created a perfectly new, enchanting civilization and even the least imaginative girls were drawn in, hanging on to every word.

Nobody noticed the bell and nobody noticed Madhu Madam re-enter.

Then all hell broke loose.

She shouted at the girls and got them back to their seats where neglected open lunch boxes sat, and then turned to Rani. 'What do you think you are – a queen with all your subjects around you? Can't solve maths problems and yet can spin all the yarns when you want to. Come here and hold out your hands.'

Rani went to her while the teacher took out the dreaded cane from the cupboard. Then the poor Madhu caned Rani with all her fury – fury at her husband, at the other woman, at the whispering neighbours and sniggering relatives and her own sorrow of feeling abandoned and anchorless. She caned Rani's palms, knuckles, arms, shoulders and even her calves. She brought down the cane again and again till she was spent.

Angry welts appeared on Rani's skin and silent tears of humiliation and injustice poured down her face.

Rani did not say a word to anyone at school or home about the incident, but after that day, she had refused to go to school anymore. Her father had tried his best to coax her into going, asked her the reason, mentioned that she could go to some other school if she was unhappy there but day after day, Rani had just continued to shake her head in silent refusal till he had to give in.

Three

On his way back home that evening, Mahesh thought of the much easier day Rani must have had in the air-conditioned beauty parlour she worked in, talking nonsense with the other girls. He did not know when the resentment had crept in, for he had always had a soft spot for his little sister. But now he had begun to compare his days, his sleep, his food with everyone else's, feeling vaguely cheated by the world that had once seemed so promising.

He heard the familiar sounds of television and raised voices when he wheeled his bicycle into the courtyard. Bittu was probably being yelled at, he thought. Most likely by Neelam. She had become short-tempered lately. She seemed constantly worried about the household budget, about Bittu's future and their own, about the constant lack of money. And this had made her irritable. Mahesh sometimes could not relate her to the shy, doe-eyed bride who had come into his home thirteen years ago. She had been nineteen, he twenty-one. How different they had been then!

The voices stopped. The television blared on. A frog croaked. Mahesh stared up at the sky. A starry night. Then he turned and entered his home. Dheeraj sat in his chair and Rani sat cross-legged on a mat, shelling peas, while Bittu lounged close by, attempting to draw a school with a black crayon.

He had only drawn yards of menacing-looking barbed wire enclosing the school so far.

Neelam sat sewing a button on one of Bittu's shirts. She repaired and darned and stitched constantly, trying to make clothes last as long as possible.

Mahesh was greeted raucously by Bittu who felt secure today. It was one of the rare days when no complaint was going to be made to his father. Mahesh sank down on a low wooden stool and took off his slippers, waiting for Neelam to fetch him a glass of water. The thought of having to now drag himself to the bathroom, fill the plastic bucket with water, bathe and dress in clean clothes exhausted him. But he had to get the stink and grime off. He leaned back and closed his eyes. From behind his closed eyelids, he could still hear the power loom whirring away. He could still see it working back and forth, back and forth.

The voices of his family washed over him. The television channels switched rapidly between two Hindi films. Rani and Bittu were fighting over the remote control, Rani deftly keeping her plate of shelled peas unspilled. A romantic duet was playing on Rani's preferred channel. Bittu kept changing it to a film that was showing a scene in a villain's den. It had a water tank full of crocodiles into which the villain threw his enemies.

'Tsk, you have no idea how much time you waste over this rubbish,' Dheeraj interrupted them. 'Now listen to this, these lines I am reading. They were said by Swami Vivekananda.'

The two promptly pressed the mute button on the television and turned to Dheeraj, as if he were another channel.

Dheeraj read carefully in Hindi, in a deliberate voice, 'Never think there is anything impossible for the soul. It is the greatest heresy to think so. If there is sin, this is the only sin – to say that you are weak, or others are weak.' Dheeraj looked up after reading this, his face looking lost and hopeful.

Mahesh leaned forward in an abrupt movement and opened his red-rimmed eyes, 'What *are* you teaching them, Papaji?' His voice was impatient, tinged with anger.

Dheeraj looked taken aback. 'But Vivekananda himself said ...'

'I don't care who said what,' Mahesh interrupting, his voice rising. 'What does it even mean? How is my thinking that I am not weak going to help my soul? Or my stomach? No matter what I make myself think, Charan Das is not weak, no factory owner I know of is weak, and I am weaker than them and I always will be.'

Mahesh had risen to his feet now, agitated. Neelam stood by him with a glass of water. He paid no heed to either.

'Look around. Open your eyes. All this you read and say is utter rubbish. You want to know the truth? The only truth I know is that there are big men and there are small men. And then there are such minuscule, tiny men that they are not even there. Zero Men. Right now we are the small men. But there is just *this* much,' Mahesh held up his hand and made a tiny space between thumb and forefinger, 'just this much stopping us from becoming those invisible, minuscule men who die quietly in misery. The zero men. There is a thin line on which we are tottering right now. And you can't even see that! One has to fight to survive.'

Dheeraj was the first to break the silence in the room. 'Calm down, son. Please. I did not mean to ...'

'When you were kicked out of your job all those years ago, at that time had you not been weak, had you tried to speak up, to ask for your rights, then maybe ...'

Mahesh stopped. The old, silent accusation hung in the air.

Dheeraj had worked as an accountant in a large general store in Guru Bazaar. He had spent thirty-two years there, carefully going over figures with a ledger and fountain pen. And then, within a space of one day, he was told that the store had been sold and he would have to leave. A supermarket came up there. Dheeraj went to see it. There were bewildering shopping baskets and trolleys, shiny-red counters and colourfully packaged food displayed on racks, and there were smiling youngsters in red uniform and matching caps bustling around. Around their necks they wore a card with their name and a paper medal that said, 'May I help you?'

They certainly could not help Dheeraj.

He had not even been allowed a month's notice. The younger assistants who had worked in the general store were put in charge of stocking and transporting, but Dheeraj was of no use now. He had to go.

He had tried to find another job but failed. He was too old to start afresh. He had some savings but the family knew they could not live on the limited amount forever.

✧ ✧ ✧

Mahesh had always loved messing about with wires and plugs and power outlets. He loved the final magic he felt when he was able to make or fix a circuit, a tenuous connection that set things alight and whirring and functioning. He had badly wanted to be an electrician. He was halfway through his two-year training as an electrician.

When Dheeraj lost his job, Mahesh had to quit and find work in a shawl factory.

Mahesh shared his bitter disappointment only with Satish, of Satish Electrical Works in their neighbourhood. Satish was a couple of years of years older than Mahesh. They had grown up playing together in the same street. Satish had promised Mahesh that he could join him after his training was over. Both had looked forward to working together. They'd spend ages trying to decide on a new name. They were toying with names like 'Bright Electricals' and 'Hare Krishna Electricals'. The latter was a suggestion from Satish's mother, with whom he lived in a small one-room house on the other side of the street, and who was an avid Krishna devotee.

But it had remained Satish Electrical Works and Mahesh had plodded on his bicycle past it to the old, dingy factory everyday, his heart heavy with unfulfilled wire-and-motor dreams.

✧ ✧ ✧

An hour later, the tension still hung tight in the house. It wasn't the first time this topic had come up, but both Dheeraj and Mahesh always managed to control themselves so it had never escalated into anything very ugly. However, on such days or evenings, after the mention of the old wound, Dheeraj would remain depressed, Mahesh angry and remorseful.

Now, everyone moved and spoke warily. But when they sat down to dinner, Bittu could no longer restrain himself.

'I have a role in a school play,' he announced importantly.

'What play?' Rani asked.

'Ramlila this year.'

'Oh,' Neelam said, with a rare spark in her eyes, looking up from the dish she was serving dal out of. 'What are you going to be, Lord Ram?'

Bittu studied his palm. 'Not exactly,' he said.

'What do you mean "not exactly"? Either you are, or you aren't.'

'It is not final yet. I'll tell you when it is final. We have to stop after school each day for rehearsals. I'll get hungry, Ma. Pack me a little something extra everyday, okay?' he said nonchalantly.

'We'll see,' Neelam said.

The next morning, Neelam packed an extra roti, some lime pickle and two glucose biscuits for Bittu. He had never before gone to school as happily as he did today, swinging his school satchel and singing.

Just before he had left, Neelam had said, 'Just don't start thinking you are Amitabh Bachchan.'

Four

Eve's Beauty Parlour had a regular subscription to several magazines. They arrived packed in cellophane at the beginning of every month and were stacked attractively in magazine racks, within easy reach of any weary woman who might be waiting for hair to set in curlers or a sandalwood face pack to harden. The girls had an unending interest in these magazines, an interest that Asha did not approve of. In the four years that she had worked at Eve's, Rani had become addicted to *Filmfare*. There would also be issues of *Femina*, *Woman's Era* and occasionally *Savvy*. Navpreet treated every *Woman's Era* issue as her own. After trying to persuade the girls that the magazines were not for them and that they should remain glossy and new-looking for the customers, Asha had reached an unspoken agreement with the girls. After a magazine became two or three months old, the girls could take them home. The claiming of ownership and the final distribution and taking turns was an elaborate process, involving delicate negotiations in which many factors were considered. Rani often got to take *Filmfare* home and those were the best evenings she had, when she'd go home, make herself a large cup of tea, take out a boondi laddoo from a jar in the kitchen and spend a pleasurable hour devouring the three.

However, a complication had arisen lately. Kavita had started to compile what she called an 'album'. Kavita's album was a fat notebook with thick, ruled pages. She collected photographs of Katrina Kaif, her favourite film actress, cut out from old film magazines and the fluff pages of newspapers. These she lovingly sorted and arranged and then pasted into this notebook with foul-smelling glue. Last week, carried away by the fervour of her hobby, Kavita had let herself be tempted to cut out pictures of Katrina Kaif from some fresh magazines, hoping that nobody would notice. But a couple of days later, Asha had discovered the peaches-and-cream-complexioned, blank-looking Katrina Kaif unceremoniously cut out from the cover story of a brand-new *Filmfare* issue. In a temper, Asha had forbidden them to touch the magazines ever again. This had dampened everyone's spirits, even though they knew that the diktat held only till Asha's temper cooled. They were all used to Asha's frequent mood swings that were sometimes irritating and at other times endearing.

'You would think I had waxed someone's eyebrows off, the way she carried on,' Kavita said.

It was Rani's secret ambition to have a similar Shahrukh Khan album. Only, she aimed for slightly better quality than Kavita did. She had collected only four pictures so far after careful selection. Asha lined the shelves with old editions of the *Times of India*, Amritsar edition. Rani scanned the city supplement pages for these whenever she went to any cupboard. She had also got two out of an old *Filmfare*. So far, she had managed to collect one picture of him at a party, in a satiny black coat, with his arm around his wife. His wife had lovely, glossy hair and wore a purple off-shoulder dress. This fascinated Rani – both the public display of affection and the bare shoulders of his wife. Rani couldn't imagine Mahesh being very happy if Neelam left her shoulders uncovered and went around smiling at people. In fact, she remembered that when they were newly-weds, he had forbidden her to wear the sleeveless blouse that she had got with one of her saris.

On the whole, Rani thought, Shahrukh Khan was definitely pleasanter than Mahesh.

The second picture in her collection was a still from *Om Shanti Om*, with Shahrukh Khan wearing a miner's helmet, his bare, wet torso gleaming and yet Rani fancied, that even in that hero-like pose, his eyes looked kind. Two more pictures, both close shots, where he looked into the camera so intensely with his deep brown eyes that Rani went melty-legged every time she looked at them. She had decided to collect at least twenty before she started pasting them.

To make an album, Rani had traded a plate of hot paneer pakoras with Bittu for a new exercise book of his. Both fervently hoped that Neelam wouldn't notice.

Today the new magazines had arrived. Rani and Kavita looked at them longingly but they were learning to be patient, to bide their time.

The Magazine Day was becoming a character-building exercise.

✧ ✧ ✧

'Where is Papaji?' Rani asked that evening when she entered the house.

A strange something flickered over Neelam's face and she replied, 'He has gone out. To the Golden Temple.' Then she added significantly, 'Even though we are not Sikhs.'

Rani clicked her tongue impatiently. 'Bhabhi, don't be ridiculous. Doesn't he go to the Shiv temple often enough? Besides, lots of Hindus go to the Golden Temple. So many. Even Kavita's father did after their bus had an accident and everyone escaped unhurt. And outsiders from Bihar and South India and all. And even foreigners.'

'Foreigners are different,' Neelam said tolerantly. 'They do all sorts of things. But Father ... well, the Golden Temple is okay, but ... but he also goes to the Pir Baba shrine every Friday. A Muslim place?'

'Why are you so upset? Let him,' Rani said, noticing that there were new frown lines on her sister-in-law's forehead.

'Rani, I just feel that gurudwaras are still okay, but Pir Baba? Muslims?' Then Neelam added, in a faltering voice, 'Savitri's husband, Rakesh, was saying that Papaji must be a strange sort of a Hindu.' Neelam looked visibly upset.

Rakesh was the head of the family next door. He was the eldest of Seema's brothers, Savitri was his wife, Karan their son. Rakesh was a pompous man, active in the community, part of many committees and associations. Rani found him intensely irritating. Seema's other brother was Harish, a slightly quieter man than Rakesh, married to a noisy, cheerful woman called Chitra. Together, the large family next door managed to create a lot of chaos, talk and gossip. However, they were also always ready to help their neighbours.

Rani put an arm around Neelam. 'Never mind what people say. Don't you have enough to do with all the work at home and with that Bittu that you are worrying about these silly things too?'

Neelam did not answer. Rani gave her another hug.

Neelam smiled faintly but did not look very comforted.

✧ ✧ ✧

That night, though Rani was tired, Bittu kept asking for a story. She refused. He badgered her. Defeated, Rani began,

> 'Once, a large green frog lived in a decorative pond in a large garden of a bungalow in Amritsar. The pond had been built by a modern architect to make the house and the garden look classy, like in foreign magazines. But the people remained the same. The pond did not make the people classy, the same way as nothing can change you from being a monkey.'

Bittu protested mildly but snuggled up to her again. Rani continued,

> 'So the pond had gone to rack and ruin, part of its marble border broken, covered in algae, the earth around it slimy. And that is how the frog liked it because that is what he considered normal ponds to be. And then, a snake came to live in the garden. The frog was completely stressed out. He knew the snake could make short work of him. If only the occupants of the house would notice this snake. They had a little child. They were sure to kill the snake. Humans were very quick in these matters. They wouldn't bother to find out if the snake was poisonous or not. But how could he bring the snake to their attention? They hardly knew of his, the frog's existence. They

stayed indoors most of the time, sitting still in front of boxes for hours on end as if hoping for a fly to come out of the box.'

'Boxes? You mean televisions?' Bittu asked intelligently.

'Yes,' Rani said.

'They must have been really stupid. How could a fly come out of the television?'

'You are the one who is stupid,' Rani said. 'The frog thought a fly would come out. The people did not.'

Both of them stared at each other in the semi-dark, having lost track of the story.

Then Rani began again,

'The frog spent many days worrying. He grew thin; he took potions made out of mashed insects to make himself stronger. He tried yoga but nothing helped. The fear of the snake made him thin and feverish.'

'How did he do yoga?' Bittu asked curiously.

'He just stood on his head,' Rani answered shortly before he could say anything else and continued,

'And then one day when the frog was squatting, completely depressed, his nerves totally shattered, he looked up to see the snake directly in front of him, just a few inches away from his face.'

Bittu gasped. Rani paused dramatically, then resumed,

'The snake said to the frog in a melancholic voice, "When I moved here, I thought I would finally get friendship and affection. But you know how I feel? I feel like weeping day and night. Why do you avoid me?"

The frog looked at the snake, not knowing whether to hop for his life or to sit there making conversation politely. But the snake continued to speak. He had worked himself up into an emotional state.

"It is not even hibernation season. And yet people won't be neighbourly or friendly. I am a young snake. Even I want some fun and laughter in my life." His voice had risen into a high pitch and he seemed close to tears. "I know that you have been avoiding me. At least don't deny it now. Don't, please don't. Let me retain some of my faith." The frog, by now, having regained his composure partially, finally replied, trying to phrase his answer somewhat delicately, "Well you see … um … I thought that you might be …". The snake interrupted sharply, "Don't hem and haw, okay. Just tell me directly."

"I thought you might want to eat me," the frog said abruptly.

The snake stared at him. There was silence for a full minute. The snake struck a tragic pose and said, "Nobody understands me." He sighed. "You see, once my mother fell really ill. She had typhoid. I prayed to Lord Shiv's snake that if she lived, I would live only on insects and beetles. And by Naag Devta's grace, my dear old mother survived, though the illness left her weakened. And a little bad-tempered. I would bring her tasty beetle curry with rice and she would fling it away saying it was no good, that I was no good, that she might be dead anyway and that the whole trouble began when she met my father."'

Bittu went into hysterical giggles at this. Rani tried shushing him but he just couldn't stop.

'Mad,' he said. 'Mother and son both.' Rani yawned, feeling very sleepy. She needed to wrap up the story quickly.

'So the frog and the snake became friends finally. The frog grew extremely fond of the snake. And yet one small tiny part of him would not trust the snake's vow not to eat frogs. It is stressful to have a friend on whom you always have to keep an eye. The frog died in a year after having a heart attack.'

Rani finished quickly, pulling her sheet up. 'Now go to sleep.' Bittu hugged her, kissed her ear and began to drift off to sleep. 'Can frogs have heart attacks?' he asked sleepily, after a while.

Rani remained silent, her eyes closed, pretending to be asleep already.

The moonlight flooded the room. A mouse peeped out of a mouse hole and scurried to the kitchen, hoping to find leftovers for his large family. Soon, Rani and Bittu were actually asleep. The only sound in the room was the whirring of the fan and the even breathing of the two. After a while, the mouse returned with bits of roti from the kitchen and disappeared down its hole again, its anxiety ended, at least for the day.

Five

Asha sat at the reception, biting her nails and looking worried, staring intently at the Laughing Buddha that sat there. She had placed him there because he was supposed to bring good luck and prosperity. At least, that was what her friend Sheetal's feng shui book said. But so far, it did not seem to be working. She was behind on the rent again. The bill for the new salon chair was still unpaid. It was an expensive one, but Asha hoped it would raise the tone of her parlour. Maybe she should change the curtains too ... Asha's thoughts trailed off to similar worries before turning to the girls she employed. They could, even the best of them, be trials. It was important that these girls be reasonably well turned out. That gave confidence to the clients that they were in good hands. Yet, after the girls had been instructed and trained in the skills of nail painting, hairdressing, make-up and were encouraged to practice it on themselves as well, it took only a couple of days for them to turn vain and self-absorbed. At times, Asha would even find a girl neglecting a client and gazing at herself in one of the mirrors, adjusting a few strands of her hair, a dreamy half-smile on her face.

Her friend Sheetal sat with her with a sympathetic look on her face and the two talked in low voices. Rani couldn't help hearing them though. She was at the sink near them, cleaning the pedicure equipment.

Asha was biting her nails again. 'I don't know what to do.

Everything goes in the rent, on paying salaries and on supplies. There are so many bills.'

Sheetal pulled Asha's hand away from her mouth. 'Look at the state of your nails. Look Asha, you want to expand and improve, I understand, but you are trying to do too much too soon.'

Asha went on feverishly, without appearing to have heard Sheetal. 'The new styling chair was expensive, but I want good, classy customers.'

Rani listened to their talk absently. The new city edition of the *Times of India* lay on the table and on the front page Shahrukh Khan smiled, his dimples showing. Rani hoped the two women would move away soon so that she could get hold of that newspaper and get a clipping. But Asha and Sheetal continued to sit there, sipping tea and talking for another half hour. Rani felt sulky and finally had to go and attend on a nervous girl, who had to be readied for bride viewing for matrimonial purposes.

'It shouldn't look like she has much make-up on. Just natural,' her mother insisted. Sheetal patted Asha's shoulder and left, carrying another book on feng shui under her arm. Asha looked at her receding back with a mix of affection and resentment. Sheetal was married to a very well-to-do businessman. Asha had been widowed ten years ago and had no rich relatives.

After the post came in and Asha had been through it, her mood became even more pensive. She tried to be cheerful with all the customers but the girls could sense she was strained. And they could sense trouble for themselves. After the last customer had left, Asha took a deep breath. 'I want all of you to come here and listen to me. I need to talk to you.'

Navpreet sighed resignedly. This infuriated Asha. Why was she sighing when she didn't even know yet what Asha had to say?

Kavita nodded vigorously. 'Coming,' she said cheerily, going to the sink to wash her hands. Asha felt her brow tighten. No sense of respect in that girl. Or of any seriousness. Ever! And Rani was looking interestedly out of the window, even smiling faintly. 'What is funny, Rani?' Asha snapped.

'Nothing. Just this woman nagging her husband, there, by that shoe shop, it looks like ...' Rani said, pointing, but with a look at Asha's face, her voice trailed off.

'All of you, here,' Asha said, clapping her hands. Finally all the girls shuffled by her side.

'Dolly, stop examining your nails,' Asha snapped.

Dolly hurriedly clasped her hands together and looked at Asha respectfully.

Asha folded her arms and tried to speak firmly, hoping they wouldn't hear the tremor in her voice. 'What is that?' Asha asked, pointing towards the bathroom.

The girls looked at her blankly.

No one dared answer. It was the bathroom, the toilet, whatever she might want to call it. But what was the catch?

'The bathroom?' Kavita ventured bravely.

'I am asking – what do you see there?' Asha's voice rose an octave higher.

Rani began to feel upset. She did not like raised voices. And there had been too many of them around her lately.

'Um ... the sink?' Kavita ventured. 'Oh, I scrubbed that thoroughly this morning.' Everyone else kept quiet and they knew Kavita should shut up, but she never knew when to.

'The lights!' Asha almost shrieked, getting to her feet. 'The lights are on. Both of them. The one on the wall as well as the one over the sink. And who is using them? Nobody.'

Asha took a deep breath.

'Who switched on these lights last?'

Nobody answered. They tried to hang their heads down and look ashamed, hoping this would blow over soon.

Then Kavita spoke. 'That woman, the one who skips like a goat each time you coat hot wax on her legs.'

'Do not speak of the customers disrespectfully. And if you knew she had switched them on, you could have switched them off,' Asha snapped back at her.

Asha waved the electricity bill in front of their faces. 'Look at this. All of you are just interested in your salaries; I am the one who has to deal with everything else. Look at this bill.'

'There is the geyser. And the hairdryers,' Mani said matter-of-factly.

'But even then, things are too, too lax around here,' Asha said. 'If I ever see any girl leaving a light or a fan on when not required, out she goes. At that very moment. I treat you people like my family, but you have no sympathy for me,' Asha ended, her imperious employer manner suddenly turning into that of a poor, misunderstood relative.

Navpreet began making consoling noises and Shama offered to make Asha a cup of tea before leaving. Rani felt disoriented. Were they just supposed to be more careful about the bills? Or be more kind in their manner? Or provide Asha emotional support since she was a widow? Rani felt out of place. She never knew what people wanted, and what they meant when they said what they said. She silently resolved that she'd make sure she switched off all the electrical appliances in the parlour after use, and with that she took off her apron and departed for the day.

✧ ✧ ✧

On Sunday morning, Neelam decided to make puris for breakfast for a treat. Bittu made several trips to the kitchen while she was cooking.

'Is it going to be potato curry or chana with the puris?' he enquired.

'Potato curry,' Neelam replied.

'Don't forget to put some imli in. I like it sour,' he said.

'Get out,' Neelam said briskly. But she said it smilingly. Rani offered to help but was instructed to collect the washing from the line and fold it instead.

When everything was ready and only the puris remained to be fried, Neelam came out of the kitchen and took out the good plates, the white ones with pink roses around the edges. There were only four of them, but a steel plate would do for Bittu. She was about to go back into the kitchen when she spotted Mahesh's shirt hanging on a hook on the wall. A corner of a bill poked out of the shirt pocket. Neelam prised it out and opened it. Even though she couldn't read much, she knew it was the electricity bill by the familiar Punjab State Electricity Board logo on it. She flattened it out and her eyes scrolled down to the figure at the bottom of the page.

₹2270.

Neelam stared at the bill unseeingly for a moment and then checked again, scanning each number. Yes, it was a staggering ₹2270.

Neelam felt her face go hot at the thought of that amount to be subtracted from the household expenses. The roof leaking, Bittu constantly outgrowing his clothes and now this! She felt she could not bear things for another moment. Rani came in, humming, '*Tujhe dekha to yeh jaana sanam*.'

She caught sight of Neelam's face. Neelam gave her a look and Rani stopped humming. 'Bhabhi, is something wrong?'

Neelam did not reply, and the by-now-familiar stony-faced look came over her. She looked out of the window and saw Mahesh wheeling his bicycle into the yard. As soon as he entered the house, Neelam beckoned him to their room, holding up the bill silently, and he followed her wordlessly into their room. Dheeraj looked uneasy but continued to read his newspaper. They could hear Neelam's voice in their bedroom, raised slightly more than normal. Though Rani and Dheeraj couldn't hear the actual words, they couldn't miss the slightly hysterical edge to her voice. Then Mahesh mumbled something. This went on for a while. Rani began to mess around in the kitchen, not knowing what to do with herself. She hated upsets in the home. For want of anything better to do, she tasted the potato curry. It was tangy and spicy, perfect for puris. Rani chopped some coriander leaves and sprinkled them over the curry.

She could hear Bittu yelling on the rooftop to Karan next door, who was on his rooftop.

Dheeraj rubbed his eyes and pinched the bridge of his nose and continued to read the newspaper in the light of the overhead bulb.

Eventually, Neelam and Mahesh reappeared. Mahesh looked strained and a little sheepish. Neelam was sniffing, her eyes and nose slightly red. Wordlessly, she went to the kitchen and turned the gas on to fry puris, as if nothing had happened. Mahesh came and sat by his father.

'How is your friend Surinder Babu?' he asked, opening conversation with his father a little awkwardly.

'Not too well,' Dheeraj said. 'He smoked all his life. He won't last long now. At least I hope not.'

Mahesh looked a little shocked.

'Better to go quickly than to linger,' Dheeraj explained briskly, folding his newspaper.

'Um ... Papaji ... Neelam is ... I mean ... both of us are a little worried.'

Dheeraj looked concerned. He looked at his son's face carefully. 'What is wrong? Is everyone okay at her parents' place?'

'Oh, yes. *They* are fine' Mahesh said quickly. 'In fact, her brothers are doing very well with their new shops.'

'Then? I hope there are no problems between you two. Just remember, she is your wife ...'

Mahesh interrupted, a little impatiently. 'It is nothing like that, Papaji. It is just that we are, I mean, all of us, are ... maybe spending too much. I mean, things are expensive – food, milk, electricity, everything has gone up and ...' Mahesh trailed away, looking uncomfortable.

'I know, son,' Dheeraj said consolingly. 'It is getting difficult in this country for people like us to live decently.' He pointed vaguely at his newspaper. 'I don't know. Is this what our freedom fighters fought for?'

Mahesh clicked his tongue impatiently.

'Papaji, forget all that for now. We just feel that ... I hope you don't misunderstand what I am saying, but we feel that everyone in the house should make an effort to save money. In every possible way.'

Dheeraj looked perplexed. 'True. That is true. But we do. I teach Bittu the value of money and Rani is such a good girl, she gives most of her salary towards the household expenses, just keeps a little for herself.'

'But look at this electricity bill,' Mahesh said. 'The lights don't need to be on all the time,' he said, pointing to the exposed light bulb overhead.

Rani saw the comprehension of what Mahesh was trying to say dawn on her father's face, saw his expression change to a slightly pained, hurt, confused one and then saw him settle back into his usual equanimous, inscrutable self.

Rani hated Mahesh at that moment.

Dheeraj was silent for a moment, looking out of the window. Then he nodded understandingly at his son. Mahesh waited uncertainly and then turned to Rani. To her, he said directly, 'Be careful of water, electricity and all. We just have to.'

Rani nodded then looked away. Mahesh left the room and disappeared into the kitchen to talk to Neelam, and soon Dheeraj and Rani could hear the couple talk in low voices.

The bill lay there on the little table, held down by a painted wooden dog of Bittu's. It looked like the one Asha had been waving in their faces last evening, Rani thought.

She suddenly felt that her world was constructed of fluttering, printed, accusing electricity bills, with last dates to pay stamped on them in red.

And that she would soon be buried under them. Rani dead under a mountain of bills, she thought.

It didn't seem fair, Rani thought, that you had to pay so much just to have light in your life.

✧ ✧ ✧

Bittu, as usual, had overheard all the conversations in the house. When they sat down to a subdued brunch of puri gone slightly cold, he piped up, 'Let us just use candles from now on.' No one spoke and Bittu dwelt on the topic further. 'And we can dress in white. The whole mohalla will be scared of us. They'll call this the haunted house.'

He was a little surprised when nobody shut him up and ate the rest of his meal in silence, knowing something was amiss.

He did not enjoy the puris as much as he usually did.

Six

'*Tujhe dekha to yeh jaana sanam,*
pyaar hota hai deewaana sanam ...' Rani sang.

It was a beautiful morning. It was one of the last of the monsoon showers. The leaves on the neem tree outside danced under the raindrops. '*Ab yahan se kahan jayein hum ...*' Rani continued happily.

'Rani Bua is a radio station who sings only Shahrukh songs,' Bittu told his grandfather. 'Even Seema Bua says so.'

'At least I can sing,' Rani shouted back. 'When you sing, it is like hyenas and donkeys are having a party together.'

'In our times,' Dheeraj said, 'film songs were beautiful. Evergreen.'

'Dadu, they are great even now,' Bittu said. You are just saying that because everyone thinks so. And actually, I've been thinking, that since I sing and dance so well, I might be able to become a very famous dancer.'

'A dancer?' Rani asked.

'Yes,' Bittu said seriously.

'What do you mean, a dancer?'

Bittu gave her a cold look.

'I mean, what kind of a dancer?' Rani amended hastily.

'The kind you see on TV. The ones who dance in good clothes in contests and people clap and then maybe you get a chance in films.'

'When you grow up?'

'No, no, very soon, very soon,' Bittu said importantly.

'Give the remote control to me,' Rani said.

'No, let us put on Aastha channel,' Dheeraj said.

'But they are showing *Baazigar*,' Rani said indignantly.

'She has watched that movie five times,' Bittu confided to Dheeraj. 'And she has to go for work, but look at her, still trying to watch one scene from it.'

Rani flung the battered remote control to them. 'Here, watch what you please.'

Dheeraj turned on Aastha channel where a benign man in a white kurta-pyjama was talking.

'Too much television will sap your brains,' Dheeraj said, when he saw that both Rani and Bittu were sulking. 'You should read good books, study well and learn to love plants. Television is just like an endless stream of performing monkeys.'

Bittu completely disregarded his grandfather.

'Dadu, you don't know anything. If someone gives you a chance in a film and you become a star, then you can have four cars in different colours and do what you please and eat what you please and nobody comes after you nagging and scolding.'

'Learn to tuck in your shirt and wipe the mud off your face first,' said Neelam, her voice slightly harsh. Bittu ignored her and continued taking huge bites of the mango pickle in his oily hand. Then he perfunctorily cleaned himself, flung his satchel over his shoulder and left for school, a frown on his usually happy face.

Rani looked at Neelam in surprise. Lately she had begun to sound different. She used to be softer when she had come into their home as a new bride. At the time, Rani had been a very young girl. She had found the whole idea of marriage, along with the accompanying shiny clothes, vanity boxes with exciting pink and brown powders in them, and the shimmering, shy bride, glamorous. Neelam had been very soft-spoken and good-natured then. She often made jokes, played Ludo with Rani and helped her make clothes for her dolls.

Slowly, over the years, just the act of living seemed to have soured Neelam slightly. Not much, but just a little.

The man on Aastha said, 'We are trapped in a cycle of craving and aversion.' Dheeraj listened to him with complete absorption.

Rani hummed to herself in the mirror, '*Teri baahon mein mar jayein hum*,' touched up her eyes with kajal again and took her purse.

'Okay Papaji, eat your meals on time,' she said to her father.

Dheeraj raised a hand in farewell and Rani sailed out of the house.

On her way to work, she as usual passed Satish Electrical Works and glanced in. Mahesh was also there, bent over a table fan, having stopped by before going to the factory. And Rani saw Satish, in his vest and khaki pants, intently welding something, the sparks lighting up his perspiring face, which as usual was red with the heat, covered with faint, attractive stubble. Rani blushed, and hurried on.

✧ ✧ ✧

Two weeks later, Bittu wasn't back from school even by four in the evening. Neelam sat at the doorstep sewing buttons onto Mahesh's shirts, looking up towards the end of the street anxiously again and again, hoping to see the familiar sight of a grimy Bittu coming home. She was beginning to worry.

After fifteen minutes or so she spotted a classmate of his, Golak, the son of Somnath of Somnath Tailors. His face and hands were filthy and part of a cobweb hung from the tip of his nose.

He was walking along dragging his shoes in the dust, a finger shoved up his nose. She called out to him. 'Ai Golak, take that finger out.'

Golak took it out and scowled at her.

'Have you seen Bittu?' Neelam asked.

Golak answered dispassionately, 'He is still at rehearsal.'

Curious, Neelam asked him, 'What role has he got in the Ramlila?'

Golak was now closely examining the finger he had taken out of his nose.

Absently, he answered, 'He is one of the monkeys in Hanuman's army, the Vanar Sena.'

Neelam was furious. She did not know at whom. At Bittu for being a mere monkey and on top of that giving himself airs about it, or at the school authorities for not giving her precious son the role of the venerable Lord Ram himself.

That evening, when she asked Bittu about it in front of the whole family, he said with great dignity, 'I am still the best actor in the whole play. The boy who is playing Ram is just more fair-skinned than me. That's all. It takes a lot of talent to be a monkey who does nothing for two hours.'

After that, nobody mentioned it again.

✧ ✧ ✧

The next day, when Rani reached the parlour, a box of sweets lay open on the reception table and Asha was beaming. The other girls stood by, a smile plastered on each face.

Shama gave a giggle. Rani smiled but before she could ask anything, Shama suddenly hopped twice on both feet, ran to Rani and hugged her. 'Guess what?'

'What?' Rani said.

'You tell, you tell.' Shama said to the others.

'Tell me what?' Rani said, her own excitement rising.

Navpreet gave Rani a broad smile.

Finally, Asha said, 'Here Rani, have a laddoo, our Anarkali is getting married.'

'Anarkali' was the nickname that had been given to Kavita, who considered Anarkali kurtas the height of fashion. And then Rani spotted Kavita, whose usual saucy, careless expression had been replaced by a shy blush and a radiant smile. Rani gave a shriek of delight and flung herself on Kavita. Then Asha broke off a bit of laddoo and fed it to Rani. Rani and Kavita fed each other some and there were lots of embraces till everyone got teary-eyed.

Then Asha beamed up at them again. 'And there is another bit of good news.' The girls looked at her expectantly.

'There are some girls from a dance troupe in Chandigarh, coming to Amritsar for a competition. Mrs Mehra put in a word for us, and this is the parlour in Amritsar, our parlour,' she added proudly, 'where they will all get ready. Facials, make-up, dressing, hairstyling, everything. Not just good money but, if we are lucky, we might even get publicity.'

Kavita and Shama clapped, and you could see joy on each face.

'So girls', Asha said standing up, her face looking softer and younger today, 'let us work hard and show them that we are the best. And Kavita, I hope your husband turns out to be a very loving man and you have a very happy life together.'

At this unlikely event of herself being happy with a stranger, Kavita shrieked in laughter and sprinted to the sink to wash her hands and begin the day's work.

✧ ✧ ✧

By evening, Asha was her harried self again. The girls from the dance troupe had arrived and seemed to fill up the whole of the parlour. It turned out that most of them did not want facials; they just wanted their saris draped in a particular way, their faces made up and their hair done for their stage performance. Asha knew it would still be a good hefty bill and was consoled by that. But the regular customers looked neglected and disgruntled – some even left in a huff – and the girls from the dance troupe themselves were quite particular and exacting.

'Don't use that foundation,' a girl squealed at Mani. 'What is it? What is it?' she said, her hand placed dramatically over her heart.

'Madam, we use only good-quality stuff.' Mani said.

'No, no, no! I have brought my Revlon foundation. Please use that,' she said.

Mani said calmingly, 'Yes, yes, we will use Revlon only.'

Another girl had hysterics, saying that her left eyebrow looked different from the right one. 'Totally different,' she said, her voice trembling.

It took Asha twenty minutes to restore the balance, to remove one hair from this eyebrow, one from that, keeping up a flow of convincing words. Nail paint had to be re-applied for four girls because they imagined that the audience would be able to see the slight smudges.

The proceedings were suspended for another twenty minutes when a girl announced that she had lost her cellphone. All her companions and all the girls at Eve's spent the next twenty minutes looking for the cellphone. They could not locate it by calling on her number since it was on silent mode. Finally, she located it in the inner pocket of her handbag.

The parlour usually closed at six in the evening, but today, the dancers left at seven in time for their show at eight. They left – eye-shadowed, faces and hair glittering and silky – waving goodbye to the girls and set forth for their performance with angelic faces that looked as if they had never troubled anyone.

Bone-tired, the girls wrapped up for the day, hardly speaking to each other. Asha sat on a chair counting the day's takings, having swallowed two aspirin with water. Navpreet brewed a huge pot of tea for everyone, which each of them gulped down in silence, and then they all left.

✧ ✧ ✧

While Rani was hopping over mud-filled potholes on her way home from work, her eyes fell on a glittering stall hung with trinkets. She spotted a pair of earrings that were shaped exactly and elaborately like bells. The kind of bells that hung in temples. She forgot her fatigue and stood poised by a pothole, not wanting to jump till she had taken a closer look at the earrings. She then casually sauntered up to the stall. 'How much are these?' she asked, trying to feign indifference. The stall owner, a scruffy boy of about eighteen, wore a bright green T-shirt that said 'I love New York'.

'Fifteen,' he answered quickly.

Rani felt relieved. She could afford that, and it sounded like a reasonable price.

However, she sneered at him out of habit. 'Fifteen? For those? Gold, is it?'

The boy ignored the jibe and said laconically, 'Twelve for you.'

'Ten,' Rani said.

The boy nodded without making eye contact with her and

started to wrap up the earrings in a bit of newspaper while he eyed a passing housewife in a red-sequined salwar-kameez.

Rani handed over a ten-rupee note and eagerly unwrapped the earrings. She put them on right there and immediately felt like a princess. Bells – a change from the usual flowers and stars! She politely waited for a stray puppy to jump over the pothole and then followed him. The puppy nosed around in a paper bag for food. The housewife in red blew her nose loudly into her pretty sequined chunni and Rani scampered home happily.

✧ ✧ ✧

'Aren't those earrings new?' Neelam asked sharply. Rani nodded, looking guilty. Neelam said nothing but she pursed her lips and continued to stir the khichdi she was making. Bittu came in and peered into the pot.

'Get away. Do you want to eat it raw?' Neelam snapped at him.

He slunk away and Rani felt a stab of pity for the forlorn-looking figure. But then he turned and gave her a broad wink. Rani smiled. Then she looked warily at Neelam. Only yesterday Mahesh had spoken about economy and today she had bought these earrings. The earrings suddenly felt stupid, frivolous. Who wore bells in their ears anyway? Rani lost all her joy in them. She took them off surreptitiously and put them away.

Her feet ached after the long day and she felt a pricking of tears at the corners of her eyes.

Seven

Bittu had been in a state of high excitement all day. It was the festival of Dussehra, the day Lord Ram had supposedly killed the demon Ravan. It celebrated the triumph of good over evil. Rani had promised to take him to see the annual burning of Ravan's effigy at Company Bagh that evening. His excitement had made him run giddily around the house, crashing into things, bumping his head and finally colliding with his mother who happened to be carrying a jar of lime pickle. The jar broke, the oil spread over the floor and Bittu was smacked on the head.

'You are getting more and more spoilt every day. No one in this house seems to think of disciplining the child. Anyone who sees you will think that your mother has taught you nothing.'

Bittu, who had hardly felt the smack, tried to pick up one of the pickle pieces scattered on the floor, not even pretending to listen to his mother.

Dheeraj spotted him, 'Stop, silly boy, there are bits of glass in the pickle.'

'Oh, the glass I am leaving on the floor,' Bittu answered reassuringly.

'Don't be foolish. You are always doing dangerous things like that. You'll hurt yourself one day. Where is your common sense, boy? Now, leave all of that alone,' Dheeraj said. He lived in constant terror of Bittu doing himself serious injury one day.

Neelam hustled Bittu towards the kitchen tap for a wash, saying in a low voice, 'The boy is not all that bad, that he needs to be shouted at so much.' There was reproach in Neelam's voice towards people who did not understand the precious Bittu she scolded all day long.

Rani saw her father's face fall.

Bittu reappeared after a while from the kitchen with wet hair and a shining face. He smiled at Rani and Dheeraj, and turned head over heels on the concrete floor.

'Fine,' Rani said, 'Be a monkey and break your neck. Then I will take Karan along to see Ravan burn instead.'

'I asked Karan already; they are all going to see the Chheharta grain market Ravan. Ma wouldn't let me go with them because of something his aunt said about someone's earrings.'

'What *are* you talking about?' Rani said.

Bittu rushed to Dheeraj, gave him a bear hug, turned two more cartwheels and ignoring Rani, sped out of the house.

Dheeraj smiled indulgently after him. 'He is a good boy. Just high spirits. I just hope he studies well. Does well at school.'

Rani turned away with guilty discomfort. Dheeraj immediately felt sorry for having brought that up.

He took a twenty-rupee note out of the side pocket of his kurta and pressed it into Rani's hand. 'Have something nice to eat this evening,' he said.

'But Papaji, I do have money.'

Dheeraj just patted her head and turned away, his mind already elsewhere.

Rani looked at the crisp new note, sighed, folded it into two and put it away in her purse.

Bittu came back in the afternoon and talked noisily throughout lunch, telling the family about what each boy in the neighbourhood would be doing that evening and how only he, Bittu would be going to see the superior Ravan burn in Company Bagh. He refused to nap after lunch and after a lot of deliberation chose a yellow polyester shirt and red shorts to wear for the special evening. He liberally sprinkled his mother's Pond's talcum powder over his person, the one she kept for very special occasions.

'You'd better look nice too,' he warned Rani.

Rani just gave him a look. Finally they left the house, Bittu clutching Rani's hand, he in his red-and-yellow outfit and she in a dainty pink salwar-kameez.

Peace descended over the house.

✧ ✧ ✧

When the ungainly auto tempo that they had boarded began to move, Bittu snuggled up to Rani. She put an arm around him and the two watched the traffic joltingly. Rani felt content.

Outside Company Bagh, Bittu eyed the balloon sellers and the aam papad vendors. 'Rani Bua,' he began. After some careful deliberation, 'You know, we could buy ...'

Rani cut him short briskly. 'If you want chaat later, you can't have anything now.'

His face fell. She said cheerfully, 'Okay, no drama. Let us go and look at Ravan and the other two.'

'Who are the other two?' Bittu asked.

'One is Kumbhkaran, Ravan's brother. He used to sleep for six months out of a year. They had to wake him up for the battle by beating drums.'

Bittu pondered over this. 'Didn't his mother say anything?' he finally asked.

'She probably did,' Rani said, 'but he was out of control.'

Bittu giggled, understanding what she implied.

'And the other?' he asked.

'That is Meghnad, Ravan's son.

'His *son*?' Bittu asked, seriously astonished now. 'But didn't Ravan stop his son from fighting like Father tells me?'

Rani felt a little confused. 'What is all this about fathers and mothers? You have come to watch Ravan burn. That is all. Give your tongue some rest now.'

'Give me just one rupee for a lollipop and I will give my tongue a rest.'

Rani didn't even bother to reply.

✧ ✧ ✧

Families milled around, the men looking harried, the women dressed in their finery and the children in brightly coloured clothes. Groups of boys and men hung around, some smoking beedis and cigarettes, disregarding the dirty looks that virtuous mothers were giving them. Rani was glad that Bittu at least remained calm and well-behaved in public. She could see several children sprinting around giddily, the way he had been doing at home.

'Let's get closer,' Bittu said eagerly to Rani. He could just see three huge painted heads from a distance and couldn't begin to imagine how wonderful the effigies would look close up.

'Okay, just don't let go my hand. I don't want to lose you in this crowd.'

'No, I won't,' he said, and clutched her hand tighter.

They edged closer, making their way through the thick crowd. Rani steered clear of groups of rowdy, leering young men and tried to find a place between a group of women with children and an excitable-looking Sikh family. Now that they could clearly see the effigies of the three demons up close, Rani and Bittu stood still.

Bittu had never seen anything so wondrous, so grand and so fairy tale-like. He could not believe that human hands had fashioned these fantastic giant figures. It was almost as if they were real demons standing still, who at any moment would come to life and slay the crowd that was scurrying around them like ants. Bittu shivered with excitement.

Even Rani was impressed.

Ravan had a superbly painted face, thick red lips, a luxuriant moustache and ten heads. All the eyes in all the heads looked ferociously at the world. The seventh head (from the right), Rani noticed, wobbled a bit. Each head wore a grand gilt crown. In one hand he raised a sword; in the other a shield. Kumbhkaran and Meghnad looked almost the same, only a little less grand, their moustaches a little less luxuriant and they had only one head each.

There was a buzz of activity around them. A tall ladder ran up to Ravan's head. An exhausted-looking man was perched on it, still adjusting the firecrackers inside. Another man, a little lower on the ladder, was quickly taking things in and out of a large bag made of stitched-up plastic sheeting and was handing them up to be put inside Ravan's head. He worked with jerky movements. He had an anxious, oily face.

After a lot of waiting and numerous false starts, a man dressed in a silk kurta-pyjama finally climbed up onto a makeshift podium a few metres in front of the effigies. The podium was made of long wooden planks that looked flimsy and the man made his way gingerly towards the microphone. But once he had the microphone in his hand, he lost all his diffidence and began shouting so loudly that nobody could follow a word. A member of the committee that he was the head of stood on tiptoe and gesticulated wildly at him, miming deafness. At this, he calmed down slightly. He began to extol the virtues not of the demons, but of the effigies that the committee had produced this year.

'We have used the best workmen and the best-quality materials. There is no Ravan in Amritsar equal to this one.' He then turned to the three effigies behind him. Pointing, he continued boastfully, '250 metres of cloth has been used, 100 quintals of paper, plain and coloured both. 200, no, 300, many, many quintals of bamboo, and many quintals of jute have been used to create these evil demons that the goodness of Ram will strike down. All this will burn today so that we can all celebrate the conquering of good over evil.' He paused for a breath. Then he spoke into the microphone again, more soberly now. 'And yes, about 7000 fireworks too.'

The excitement built up in the waiting crowd and finally, the exhausted-looking man climbed up to Ravan again for a last time, this time a faint smile on his face, holding a flaming torch of rags soaked in oil. Bittu's jaw slackened as he watched in fascination.

With a few quick manoeuvres, the men simultaneously, deftly, lit up various places in the anatomies of the three unfortunate men. Thus choreographed, the grand blaze began.

The trail of the fire was followed avidly by hundreds of eyes. First, a lone firecracker burst, revealing a hole in Ravan's leg. The crowd burst into deafening applause. There were loud bangs and bits of coloured paper went flying high into the air.

Ravan burnt and banged and blazed. Meghnad and Kumbhkaran

followed suit. Rani looked down at Bittu who was staring with open-mouthed awe, his small face entirely still.

The entire scene appeared fantastic – the blazing effigies and the hysterical crowd. Then suddenly, each of Ravan's heads began to explode one by one. And at that moment, Rani felt a flash of pain in her own head. She tried to press one palm over both her eyes, unwilling to let go of Bittu's hand. When she opened her eyes, the fireworks were still going, the crowd was still cheering. And Rani had the strangest feeling. Hundreds, maybe even thousands, of humans had gathered, had put up effigies of a man, his brother and his son, and for some wrongs that the three had supposed to have done, god knows how many years ago, wrongs that these people had not even witnessed, they were punishing them. And they were celebrating the punishment. The hatred was being carefully kept alive. It did not seem like the celebration of good conquering evil. It seemed like the celebration of savagery, of unforgiving cruelty, of harsh judgement. The festive gaiety around her suddenly seemed false. In an unreal moment of horror, Rani saw with complete clarity the scene that was being played out in front of her eyes. She could suddenly discern the difference between what appeared to be happening and what was actually happening.

Rani stood mutely in the middle of the cheering crowd. Another firecracker went off. Bittu shrieked in glee. Rani again felt a shooting pain at the left side of her head. The fire finally began to burn Ravan's face. His moustache drooped, his chin curled up and his face slowly became a sad shrivel. Rani felt sorry for him. There was a lump in her throat. Who knew who Ravan had actually been? Who knew what happened after you died? Could his spirit still see how he was put up in all his grandeur along with his brother, only to be torn down, burnt and jeered at? And his son, Meghnad, could he see the same treatment meted out to his little boy? Did anybody deserve this?

If she went by the stories Papaji read out of his newspaper and what he said about all humans having follies, if Dussehra was about burning evil and punishing follies, half the city should be busy burning themselves every Dussehra. With no crowds left to watch.

And then, Rani felt overcome and confused by her own thoughts. She looked at the sea of faces around her. She shook her head, trying to clear it. What was wrong with her? Why was there a lump in her throat? Why did she feel like crying? It was ridiculous. She hadn't even cried when Shahrukh Khan had died in *Kal Ho Na Ho*. But she remembered that even then she had had a lump in her throat that had lasted for ages.

It was just Dussehra, Rani kept repeating to herself, trying to feel normal again. It was a festival. She was supposed to be enjoying herself. She looked down at Bittu, who was straining his neck to follow the path of the beautiful flames of a rocket, his face alight with joy. Rani softened instantly at the look on his face. He caught her eye and smiled, the recent gap where he had lost a tooth showing.

The two stood there mesmerized for another ten minutes. Then the fireworks became less frequent and less spectacular. Rani bent down to Bittu's ear. 'Let's go now,' she said, 'otherwise we will never get an auto tempo back. We have to leave before the rest of the crowd.' Bittu stood hypnotized, a silly smile pasted on his face, apparently deaf.

Rani tried again. 'The chaat and samosas will probably be over if we wait any longer.' This galvanized Bittu into motion. 'Oh yes,' he said, almost in a panic, 'let us go.' They made their way outside the Company Bagh gates. After much bargaining, negotiating and compromising, Bittu bought a red balloon, a slab of aam papad, a multi-coloured plastic trumpet, an ice cream stick and the promised plate of chaat. Rani had a cup of vanilla ice cream too and despite Neelam's disapproval the other day, could not help buying a pair of red butterfly-shaped earrings. They only cost ten rupees, she told herself consolingly.

A pleasant breeze had sprung up. The pair, sticky-faced from the ice cream and completely tired, dragged their feet to an auto tempo and made their way peacefully home.

However, in one corner of her head, a corner perhaps inherited from Dheeraj, a corner that was never easily placated, Rani still felt vaguely disturbed.

Eight

It was a Wednesday morning, a cloudy one. Mahesh and Rani had left for work and Bittu for school. Dheeraj sat by the window to save electricity, reading a small book of the poet Kabir's couplets that he had picked up near the bus stand.

Neelam had just finished taking a bath and now sat alone on the bed in her tiny bedroom in a careless pose, wearing a fresh sari, her wet hair tied up in a towel. This was the only time and place where she would let her pallu slide and her demeanour relax. A picture of a rosy-cheeked, smiling baby hung over a wall. Mahesh had put it up when she was expecting Bittu and they had never got around to taking it down. This, she thought, was also a reminder of how long it had been since the house had been painted. On another wall hung a cross-stitch work depicting a thatched cottage with honeysuckle growing over it. Neelam remembered working hard at it two months before her wedding when she had been nervous, eager to please and looking forward to showing off her few skills. She had embroidered it beautifully, even though she had never seen a thatched cottage and had no clue as to what honeysuckle was. Now, the frame of the embroidery had acquired grime that no amount of dusting and polishing would remove.

A single wooden in-built cupboard in one of the walls contained all of Neelam's worldly possessions.

She had hung a small wall mirror near the window. In the early days of her marriage, she would line her eyes with kohl and then carefully make a round vermilion mark on her forehead, the kind Mahesh loved. Lately, with all the worries she had, she had stopped bothering and had begun to use Shilpa sticker bindis.

Neelam knew she had been short-tempered lately, especially with the child. But he was so naughty, so immune to all forms of discipline. Rani was nice but had the carelessness that most unmarried girls do, and Neelam dearly wished that her father-in-law would be more worldly-wise. And Mahesh, who had always been a considerate husband, lately seemed tired all the time. Either he would refuse to discuss their worries or if he did discuss them and tried to find solutions, he would seem exhausted for days after, going for long solitary walks and smoking beedis with Satish and his other friends, staying back late at Satish's shop to watch cricket matches on the small television set they had there.

Neelam sighed, got up, did her hair, put on her bindi and vermilion, adjusted her sari and went out of her room.

'Papaji,' she called in a low voice to Dheeraj, 'I am leaving for the temple. Shall I make a cup of tea for you before going?'

Dheeraj looked up from his book and said with a smile, 'No, no, I am fine. You go.'

Neelam went out, closing the door behind her, and Dheeraj went back to Kabir's poetry.

✧ ✧ ✧

Ten minutes later, the doorbell rang. Dheeraj opened the door to see a pale young man standing there, his Adam's apple showing above the buttons of his black-and-white checked shirt. He wore a glittering chain from which hung a pendant with 'Om' engraved on it.

Dheeraj tried to place him but couldn't.

'Namaste, Bauji,' the young man said, folding his hands together and bending to touch Dheeraj's feet in a single, swift motion. 'Didn't you recognize me? I am Aman,' he said eagerly.

Dheeraj's eyes lit up in recognition. 'Oh, you are Surinder's boy, aren't you?'

'Yes, I am,' he said, his hands still folded.

'Come in, come in,' Dheeraj said putting an arm around him.

'Sorry I didn't recognize you straightaway. You have grown. I used to see you fly kites while we drank tea. It all changed after Surinder fell ill. And what a long illness! It has been years. Now we hardly meet,' he said, a little despondently. 'Once or twice a week, though, I make a call to your mother, without fail, from the corner PCO. It's been difficult since you moved house. Majitha Road is too far for me.'

Aman did not appear to be listening and seemed a little ill at ease. Dheeraj noticed this and asked, 'How are you, son? Is all well?'

Aman nodded. Dheeraj went to the kitchen and fetched a glass of water for him.

'Have this and come out with me. Your Bhabhi is not at home. So we will have to go to the corner shop for tea.' Then he added with an apologetic smile, 'I still can't make a decent cup.'

Aman suddenly broke into speech. 'No, no Bauji, I do not want tea. I came to speak about a rather delicate matter.'

Dheeraj paused, waiting. But Aman just fiddled with his shiny watch.

'Yes?' Dheeraj asked encouragingly.

'It is like this. You know Father has been ill.'

'Yes, and I have high regard for your mother for taking care of him the way she does.'

'But the expenses have been high – medicines, doctor's visits. And he didn't have much saved.'

Aman fiddled with his watch again. When he looked up, Dheeraj noticed dark circles under his eyes. 'I work at a bicycle repair shop. It doesn't pay much though I work long hours. A new shop, a very small one, has come up for sale. If I could buy it ...' he trailed off. Then he took a deep breath and began again, 'If I could buy it, I could save the family from poverty and from the disgrace of debt. I have some savings, but not much. I need just a little more.'

He looked pleadingly at Dheeraj.

'If you could lend me that sum, Bauji, I will return it to you as soon as I can. I promise I will.'

Dheeraj felt pained. He did not know what to say. He had a few savings, not much, but some he had kept by for his old age. But how would his son and daughter-in-law feel if they knew he had lent his savings to someone else when they were constantly complaining of lack of money?

He wanted time to think.

Aman sank back into his chair in silence.

Dheeraj thought back to the days when he had lost his wife. Mahesh was seven and Rani three when their mother had died. She had been a doting, patient, playful mother and the children had been confused and miserable. Surinder and his wife had been by their side all the time. Though relatives had appeared helpful, none of them had actually done anything. Surinder had made arrangements for the cremation while a shell-shocked Dheeraj had wandered around the house unseeingly. He had loved his wife. In his own way.

Surinder's wife had taken care of the children without making too much of a show of it. She had taken them to her home, fed and clothed them. They had slept snuggled up to her while her own children had been convinced to give up this right for a few nights. Surinder and his wife had spoken little but done everything possible for Mahesh and little Rani. Surinder had even gone to the store where Dheeraj worked, explained things there and requested for Dheeraj's leave of absence so that he could grieve. And now that very Surinder's son was sitting in front of him asking for, what was, after all, just a loan. How could Dheeraj refuse?

Dheeraj said, 'Of course I'll help. I'll lend you the money. It is all I have.'

'I'll return every rupee, Bauji,' Aman said, almost in tears now. 'If you only knew what it has been like at home ... And the shame I would have felt at borrowing money from a stranger.'

Aman looked completely distressed now.

'Come with me,' Dheeraj said decisively. 'Do not torture yourself further. We'll go to my bank right now.'

And the two left.

When Dheeraj got back home, Neelam was waiting for him.

'Who was that boy who came here? The one you went out with? Seema next door told me.'

Resignedly, Dheeraj told her everything.

The rest of the day was a stony, silent accusation.

✧ ✧ ✧

When Rani got back home, she could sense the tension in the air. Dheeraj had a defeated air about him while Neelam looked almost as if she was grieving. It had been a rough day at work for Rani. She had massaged five pairs of feet, done four facials and threaded more eyebrows than she could count. There had also been a perm that she had to do, and the chemicals had made her eyes water. They still hurt slightly. She wished Bittu were home but he was out playing somewhere. Rani wanted to curl up with the *Filmfare* she had brought home but Neelam appeared tired. So Rani went into the kitchen to help.

'Do you have a headache, Bhabhi?'

Neelam didn't reply.

In silence, Neelam cooked dal while Rani made rotis. And then Neelam noticed that it had grown dark outside. She went to the door and looked out for Bittu. She spotted him at the street corner with two other boys, trying to climb onto a bicycle double his size.

The sight seemed to drive her to rage.

'Bittu!' she shouted. 'Bittu, come back inside.'

Bittu, who usually disregarded her, discerned a note of danger in her voice today and walked back. At the doorway, she shook him by his shoulders.

'What is all this loafing? Day in and day out. When do you study? Do you think you are a government officer's son? What is going to happen to your life?'

Bittu, a little surprised by her vehemence, which seemed stronger than her usual bad temper, said, 'But Ma ...'

'Don't talk back at me,' Neelam shouted. 'You will end up on the streets. It isn't as if anybody is saving for your future. It isn't as if you are going to get some inheritance. Yes. You will end up on the streets.'

'But Ma ...'

Neelam's voice was quivering with rage now, 'Don't talk back to me, I said.' And she slapped him hard, at the same moment that Mahesh entered the house.

Bittu looked shocked for a split second. He went still and he gazed up at his mother. Then his dusty little face crumpled up and he began to cry bitterly.

Mahesh and Dheeraj both rushed to comfort him.

'Why are you so angry with the boy?' Mahesh asked Neelam, his own voice a little angry.

'Don't ask me,' Neelam answered, in tears herself. 'It isn't as if anyone in this house asks me or consults me before doing anything. Nobody cares about Bittu's future. So what? If this is God's will, that my son should spend his life working in a mill like his father, what can I do?' Neelam wiped her tears with the pallu of her sari.

Dheeraj's face turned white. He did not speak.

Bittu was still howling. Rani tried to gather him in her arms to comfort him. Neelam walked up to them and pushed Rani away roughly. 'Now don't I even have the right to slap my child to teach him anything?' She took the wailing Bittu by his elbow and disappeared into her room with him.

✧ ✧ ✧

Mahesh quietly went into the kitchen, drank a glass of water and left to smoke some more beedis with Satish, his only refuge these days. Mahesh felt that each day that he spent working the wretched power loom in the factory was killing him slowly. His home had ceased to be the once peaceful haven it used to be. Now only the sparking, the welding, the beedis and Satish's undemanding company could give him solace.

✧ ✧ ✧

Dheeraj and Rani looked at each other, unable to speak.

'I will … um … just go for a walk,' Dheeraj said, averting his eyes. And he left.

Rani sank down on her mattress, sad. She could still hear Bittu wail.

She sat there till the sounds from Neelam and Mahesh's room had ceased. She had lost all desire to read the new *Filmfare*.

Nine

Neelam and Savitri both sat in a rickshaw dressed in their good, if not best, saris, scanning the signboards that they passed. 'Do you remember where it is?' Neelam asked anxiously.

Savitri continued to look distractedly around the crowded bazaar. 'It was somewhere here. I don't know. Should be somewhere here.' The rickshawalla overheard them and turned his head. 'What are you looking for?'

Savitri leaned forward and said, 'Pandit Dina Nath, an astrologer who used to sit somewhere here.'

'Oh, him? He makes a lot of money now with his horoscopes and planetary positions and all that rot. He has got a room on a first floor now. Above Anand Fabric Shop. I know. I will take you there.'

Savitri settled back and she and Neelam exchanged relieved glances.

The rickshaw halted in front of Anand Fabrics. A narrow door by its side revealed a dark, steep staircase. 'Pandit Dina Nath' – a yellow board proclaimed in Devanagri script. The two women paid the rickshawalla ten rupees without haggling and then gingerly made their way up the steep stone staircase, carefully holding onto the pleats of their saris.

They had to wait while the pandit spoke to a couple in a low voice. After they left he turned to them. 'Yes. And how can I serve you?' he asked, his voice comfortingly paternal. He wore a white dhoti and kurta, had a red tilak on his forehead and a red cloth thrown over his shoulder. He looked like he was dressed to play the part of an astrologer in a play or a movie.

'Namaste Panditji,' said Savitri folding her hands.

Neelam did the same awkwardly.

He just nodded back at them and motioned them to sit down.

They settled themselves cross-legged in front of him. He did not make eye contact. He looked learnedly out of a small window at the crow sitting outside. 'Which one of you is troubled, sisters?'

The crow cawed back at him.

He frowned at the crow.

The crow stared back, beady-eyed.

Savitri began, 'This is my friend. No end to her troubles. She is good and God-fearing. But,' she said in a tragic voice, 'it seems that these days that counts for nothing. You helped us once, so I brought her here.'

Pandit Dina Nath sighed wearily. 'So much trouble, so much strife. Surely this is kalyug, an evil period.' Then he consulted his gold watch and his tone became brisker. 'So what is the trouble?'

Neelam began to speak, haltingly at first, then with increasing confidence and loquacity.

She rambled on about various unconnected worries, of the dipping finances in her household, the foolishness of the menfolk in her home, a persistent backache and a headache that she had begun to get and her worries about Bittu's future.

Another crow had joined the first one now and both now looked in fixedly.

Neelam ended almost tearfully. 'It isn't as if I don't do my duties. And I go to the temple every Monday and as many other times as I can with a full thali of flowers, coconut, everything. I am just in despair now.'

Pandit Dina Nath closed his eyes and sat like that for several seconds. Then he opened them and nodded. 'How many family members live in your house?' he asked.

'My father-in-law, husband, sister-in-law and my little son, and me of course.'

'Any servants?'

'If we had been able to afford servants, would I be so troubled?'

'Besides,' she added with a touch of pride, 'we do all our own work with our own clean hands.'

'Who earns?'

'My husband. Uh ... and I suppose also my sister-in-law.'

'Does your husband drink?'

'Not a drop.'

'Does he have any other vices?'

'Not at all. He is almost like Lord Ram.' Then, checking herself from getting carried away, she said, 'Well, he does smoke. Too much sometimes. And watches cricket matches all the time.'

'Also, he doesn't listen to me half the time. And if a plumber or an electrician is to be called, he will keep putting it off till ...'

'Stop talking, woman. Those are not vices.'

Neelam stopped, looking suitably chastened.

'Are there any elders in your family?'

'My father-in-law.'

'And do you serve him well?'

'Oh yes, I do. But he is another one for doing as he pleases.'

Neelam began to study her ring moodily. Pandit Dina Nath sighed. All of a sudden, one of the crows began to caw raucously. Pandit Dina Nath got up and tried to shoo them away. Then he came and sat down again, wiping his brow. Savitri said ingratiatingly, 'Crows cawing means you will have guests.'

Pandit Dina Nath silenced her with a look.

'So,' he said, 'there will have to be a puja. 11,000 mantras will have to be read over seven days. I will have to get seven more Brahmins to do it with me. I will do it right here. It will cost you ...'

Neelam interrupted, alarmed. 'No, no, Panditji, we don't want to put you through so much trouble. Just do something at our home and give us your blessings. In one day,' she added hastily.

Pandit Dina Nath looked sulkily at the crows outside.

'Oh, well,' he said. 'Everyone wants fast methods these days. So we will have a shuddhi havan at your home. It will purify the home and the hearts of all its dwellers.'

He took out a calendar and consulted it. 'Lord Shani must be propitiated,' he said, 'so it will have to be on a Saturday. I am only free on the third Saturday of this month. Doing many Shani pujas these days.'

'And the fees?' Neelam asked hesitantly.

'We don't take fees,' he said disdainfully. 'You can give whatever your heart tells you to. According to your faith.'

Savitri quickly scrambled to her feet. 'Yes, yes, I will explain all that to her. We are grateful for your blessings.'

Pandit Dina Nath just nodded and efficiently handed them a photocopy of a computer printout of a readymade list of things they would need for the ceremonial prayer. Savitri nudged Neelam and Neelam quickly took out a hundred-rupee note from her purse and put it down in a thali that lay there for the purpose. They bowed their heads and left in haste.

When Neelam turned her head at the top of the staircase, Pandit Dina Nath, looking irritated, was still trying to shoo the crows away from his windowsill.

✧ ✧ ✧

Neelam was serving dinner. Rani had refused hers. Lately her appetite had been going down. Dheeraj and Mahesh sat cross-legged while she brought hot rotis to their plates. Bittu squatted close by, engrossed in the small television, watching a dance contest between school children. The judges were from the film industry. Two of the children were in tears for having been criticized by them.

'What is there to cry about?' Bittu said disapprovingly. Rani sat by him, darning a tear in his shorts. He was eating absentmindedly from a plate in front of him.

When dinner was almost over, Neelam said, in a nicer tone than she had been using lately, 'I went to see a very well-known panditji. Generally. To protect the health and prosperity of this home. Third Saturday of this month, he'll come to conduct a ceremony. Just a small havan. For purification.'

Mahesh looked up, angry. 'You went to a pandit? Without

discussing it with me? Don't you know they are all frauds? How much did you pay him?'

Neelam's face hardened. 'Yes. I did go to see a pandit. *Somebody* has to think about the welfare of this household.'

'Are you trying to say that I don't think about it?' Mahesh asked heatedly.

Rani interrupted, trying to calm her brother down.

'Bhabhi didn't mean that. At least listen to her. She is just ...'

'You keep out of this.' Neelam snapped at her. 'I can talk to my husband without your help.'

Rani subsided, stunned. Neelam had never spoken to her like this ever before.

Mahesh continued, oblivious to what everybody else was saying, 'Do you know what a havan will cost? And god knows how many people we will have to feed.' He turned to his father and asked fretfully, 'How many Brahmins do you think will be required to come?'

Dheeraj averted his gaze and said softly, 'I ... um ... I don't think, well, actually I won't be here on the third Saturday of this month.'

'You won't be here? What do you mean?' asked Neelam.

Dheeraj began to look harassed now. Rani noticed that his eyes were red-rimmed and he seemed to have lost some weight.

'There is this course,' Dheeraj said. 'A ten-day meditation course. I will be going there.'

Silence.

'A course? ' Mahesh asked, sounding perplexed.

'I told you ... it is a sort of ... a meditation course.'

'Where are you going, Papaji?' Rani asked.

'Dharamsala,' he answered.

'For ten days?' screeched Neelam. 'What rubbish is this?'

'It is not rubbish,' Dheeraj said quietly.

At this, Neelam slammed down the serving spoon that she was carrying on top of the television. Every head in the room turned towards her. Even Bittu couldn't ignore the proceedings now.

'I am holding a puja,' Neelam said, her voice trembling, clutching the end of her pallu tightly, her knuckles white. 'And I am doing it for the good of this home where everyone seems to think just of themselves. I have arranged everything, I have spoken to the pandit, I have invited Brahmins, I have invited our relatives and neighbours.' And Neelam burst into tears.

Before anyone could respond, she lifted an angry, accusatory face at Dheeraj. 'Both my brothers and their wives will be coming. And the elders in our house will be gallivanting in the hills, taking cool walks, while we struggle under the burden of bills and groceries.' Mahesh and Rani both stared at Neelam. She had never openly been rude to Dheeraj before, no matter how irritated or discontented she had been. She had always maintained the decorum of the daughter-in-law. This was the first time she was lashing out at him.

Dheeraj's silence and stillness seemed to incense her further. She continued, her voice rising to a higher pitch, 'The elders in other households are the backbone of their families. Already people ask me all the time why you never attend any wedding, any function. Are you not happy for other people? Having lost your wife, do you grudge other people their happiness that you don't join any celebration? You just fritter away money on strangers, embarrass us by worshipping at this mosque, going to that baba, even visiting churches. You don't bother to keep an eye on what is being spent where, and use the light bulbs and fans as if we get electricity for free.' Neelam was hysterical now, all her bottled-up resentment overflowing, her accusations growing wilder and more disconnected. 'If it weren't for you, I wouldn't be ashamed to go to gatherings, to meet relatives and if it weren't for you, I could save this household from being sucked dry.'

When she stopped, there was a deafening silence in the room.

Dheeraj slowly got to his feet, took up his walking stick and went out. Bittu crept to Rani and clung to her chunni. Neelam, her face covered with tears now, her eyes bloodshot and her breathing uneven, went into her room and slammed the door shut. Mahesh stood still for a while.

Then he too left.

Ten

The next morning, Rani felt too fatigued and listless to go to work. She considered calling Asha and taking the day off, but spending the day in the house might be even more depressing. Dheeraj wasn't in the house when she got out of bed; Bittu was still asleep by her side, hunched up like a frog. Rani dropped a light kiss on the back of his head.

Mahesh's bicycle wasn't in its usual place in the courtyard. There was silence in the kitchen, so Neelam must still be in her bedroom. Rani's head and heart were heavy.

She remembered Papaji's face when Neelam had been shouting. More than hurt, there was bewilderment on his face. As if he had just started to read a book and realized that he did not know the language.

Rani wished she could comfort him but though affectionate himself, he had always been a difficult man to comfort. Rani wondered if things would have been different if her mother had been alive. Apart from all this, her heart was full of anger against Neelam. Rani decided to get ready and leave quickly for work. If she encountered Neelam this morning, she might say or do anything. Moving quietly, Rani quickly bathed. When she came back in the room, she could hear Neelam in the kitchen telling Bittu to drink up his morning glass of milk. Rani left, shutting the door softly behind her.

At the beauty parlour, she walked into an animated discussion between Kavita and Dolly, both proclaiming equal love for Salman Khan and Hrithik Roshan.

'Rani, who do you like more – Salman or Hrithik?' Kavita asked her. Navpreet frowned at them.

'Hrithik Roshan,' Rani answered dully, dutifully scrubbing her hands with the depressing Dettol soap. She did not bother to say that, actually, Shahrukh Khan was the best. She suddenly remembered that tonight there was an interview with him on Zoom TV. She would try to get home on time. Maybe she'd feel better after watching it.

Rani's heart wasn't in her work today. She was lethargic, had a headache and was quick to lose patience. A woman whose face she was massaging kept opening her eyes. 'Madam, please keep your eyes closed,' Rani said, a little sternly, 'or the cream might get into your eyes.' The woman, who was bullied at home by her mother-in-law, quickly shut her eyes, not daring to open them again till Rani said she could.

Shama fiddled around with the radio till she got a clear channel and a romantic duet.

Rani had eaten nothing in the morning nor had she packed any lunch. But the idea of the oily bhatura-chana that was sold at a stall close by, and which all the girls loved, made her queasy today. She had just a cup of tea at lunchtime.

'No food today?' Kavita asked.

Rani shook her head.

'Fasting?'

Rani shook her head again. For a change, Kavita left her alone after that, after tentatively offering her some of her own subzi-roti, which Rani politely refused.

A little after lunchtime Navpreet called for Rani, saying there was a phone call for her. Rani went to the phone and held the receiver to her ear.

'Rani Bua?'

Rani sighed.

'It is you again. What is the matter, Bittu? You will make me lose my job.'

'No, no, I'll talk to them if they try that,' he said reassuringly.

'What do you want?'

'When you come home, on your way back can you buy me one packet of nuts and bolts, one packet of rubber bands and one hammer?' Bittu said, sounding as if he had learnt the list before calling her.

'What do you want them for?'

'I am making something. It is a secret. It is very urgent.'

Rani was about to refuse when she remembered how subdued he had been last evening with all the shouting going on. She considered his request.

'What kind of nuts and bolts?'

'Mixed sizes. Get them from Satish's shop but don't tell Father.'

Rani's heart leapt a little at the mention of Satish.

'And where does one get a hammer?'

'Bua, why are you fussing? I am not asking for gold statues. These things you can get anywhere.'

When Rani had not refused outright, Bittu had become emboldened.

'I will try. What will you do if I get them?'

'I will be always grateful to you. I will consider you the best ...'

'No,' Rani said firmly. 'Tell me something that you will actually do.'

'Oh, okay. If you have to trouble a fellow over every little thing you do for him, I will ... I will spend the next Sunday afternoon by-hearting the six-times multiplication tables, okay? Promise.'

'Okay,' Rani said. 'Let's see. I have to go now.'

'Work hard,' Bittu said patronizingly, before hanging up.

✧ ✧ ✧

'Rani,' Asha called imperiously, with one of her sudden mood changes.

Rani looked up. 'Yes Madam?'

'Was that an urgent call?'

Rani thought quickly. 'Yes Madam. My aunt has got typhoid.'

Asha looked at her disbelievingly.

'Never mind,' she said. 'I have to go out today. A man will come with a delivery. Sign for it, receive it and tell him to collect his payment later. Even if he doesn't come till six, let the other girls go, but you wait for him. Don't wait longer than seven-thirty though. Hopefully he will be here by then. Lock up and switch off all the lights before leaving. Leave the delivered package on my desk.'

Rani listened, dismayed. Now she would miss Shahrukh Khan's interview on Zoom TV. She said nothing, however.

She went off resignedly to give a deluxe pedicure to an exhausted-looking housewife whose calloused feet looked as if they hadn't been cleaned and scrubbed for years. Rani stayed bent down again over her toenails, scrubbing them thoroughly with an orange-handled brush that looked horribly, brightly cheerful.

Then she had to make up another woman's face for a formal party. Rani politely suggested that the woman, who was in her forties, wear a muted earth-coloured lipstick. But the woman, whose made-up eyes were looking lovely, was now totally carried away by vanity and insisted on a dark maroon lipstick.

Rani gave up and outlined the lips with a maroon lip liner, filling in the rest of the space with a brush. While she was doing it, the woman's face, otherwise fairly average, began to appear grotesque to Rani.

And after working intently on the mouth for five minutes, she felt as if the entire universe contained just this one maroon mouth.

And then in Rani's head, the mouth seemed to morph into Ravan's painted lips. In the same instant, the jeers made at Ravan, Neelam's unkind words to Dheeraj the previous evening and the general harshness of life, all came together inside a small place located in a remote corner of Rani's being. Dheeraj was poor Ravan and Ravan was poor Dheeraj.

All the pieces fit, made complete sense.

Total clarity shimmered through.

Then, in the very next second, when Rani tried to recollect it, it was gone. And the small, clear place inside her immediately got cluttered up again.

'I must be going mad,' Rani thought, putting the finishing touches on the woman's make-up.

The evening wore on. The parlour began to empty. Satisfied women with massaged faces, gleaming skin, scrubbed feet and painted nails began to depart one by one. The last to leave was a woman who took a beautiful glass bottle out of her handbag, sprayed herself with the perfume in it and left. The girls in the parlour began the daily ritual of wrapping up, cleaning, washing, putting away.

Kavita collected all the towels and sheets and stuffed them into the twin red laundry baskets. Brushes and combs were boiled in water. The sky grew heavy with dark clouds. Dolly brewed sweet tea in the back room and the tired girls settled themselves down. Dolly was in high spirits. In the absence of the statuesque Asha the girls grew boisterous, though Navpreet tried, not very successfully, to look stern.

One by one the girls began to leave. In the end, Rani was left alone with Kavita.

'I would have waited with you,' Kavita said, 'but I am supposed to go to the tailor with my mother. For my bride-type clothes,' she added.

Rani smiled at her. 'Have fun.'

'What fun?' Kavita said. 'My mother doesn't listen to a single thing I say. She *actually* told the tailor not to listen to me. And she has agreed to have only one Anarkali kurta stitched. She told me I wasn't Madhubala in *Mughal-e-Azam* and that I should dress like a sober, virtuous bride, not a film heroine.'

'You know,' Kavita continued thoughtfully, 'once, when my mother was clearing out a cupboard, a big tin of raisins fell on her head. Maybe that's why she talks so much nonsense.'

'Don't worry,' Rani said. 'You will look like a heroine no matter what you wear. But you shouldn't talk about your mother like that.'

Kavita giggled. 'You should hear what *she* says about me.'

After some more banter Kavita left, a visible spring in her step, and Rani was left alone, for the first time, in an empty beauty parlour.

✧ ✧ ✧

She stood in the middle of the room, not knowing what to do with herself. She coughed. The sound echoed. During the day, you sometimes couldn't hear yourself speak over the voices and the dryers.

Rani finally sat down on a chair. She conscientiously switched off all the extra lights in the parlour. The chilly November evening did not need a fan anyway. She left a single overhead light on and sat down on one of the chairs. Her face looked back at her from the mirror opposite. It was like looking at a stranger. Rani gave a half-smile to her image. The stranger seemed to smirk back. Rani continued to stare.

All human faces were a little strange, she thought, with their protrusions and orifices. Ears especially, come to think of it, stuck out strangely. Rani was struck by how all women hung earrings on them, decorating the strange convoluted protrusions. If you looked closer at ears, you actually saw lightless tunnels that led into the dark recesses of the brain, where god knows what happened and what lived.

Yes, perhaps earrings were inappropriate as a concept, or maybe they were used to camouflage the awkard shape of ears.

Rani scratched her head and leaned back. The dim overhead light was round, and there was a silly pattern of tiny stars around it. Rani had never noticed the stars before. She began to count them. She had reached sixty-four when she realized that they were in a circle and she was counting the same ones over and over again, not knowing where the circle began and where it ended.

Things could be tricky.

Rani looked at the wall clock. It was only six-fifteen.

Rani looked at herself in the mirror again. Her image seemed ineffectual, someone who had no power over any events and not even on the direction of her own life.

And she did not know about others, but a nose looked decidedly funny on her face. Rani stretched and got up. She went through the magazines half-heartedly, but she had already read them. Only one waited to be taken home by her. It had a picture of Shahrukh Khan, looking a little different from his usual self in a grey T-shirt, unkempt hair, a leaner look but with his dimpled smile still in place. Soon, hopefully, the picture would find its rightful place in her album. She gazed longingly at him for a while. He had just the kind of hair that one would want to touch or even shampoo and blow-dry.

Satish's hair was nice, not oiled and plastered to the scalp at least, but of course it could never be as good as Shahrukh Khan's, Rani thought idly.

Rani, now, put aside the magazine too. And then the thought which she had been persistently pushing into the recesses of her mind came jumping forward with leaps and bounds.

She wanted to hold her Papaji close.

The thought of him wandering around in his white kurta-pyjama, feeling insulted and disoriented and yes, lonely, though he would never admit it, tugged at her heart. She wished he were as easy to comfort and console as Bittu was.

Rani also wished she was one of the customers at Eve's Beauty Parlour and that somebody could give her the forty-five minute hot olive oil head massage. The nerves in her scalp felt like tightened wires. The workings of her mind did not make sense even to her.

She swivelled around in her chair facing away from the mirror. The dimly lit parlour looked eerie.

The helmet-like dryers used for perms looked vaguely menacing. The cubicles for facials were dark and claustrophobic. Now that all the beauty apparatus and paraphernalia was silent and in repose, the familiar shapes appeared odd, alien and pointless.

The thought that the still parlour waited like this every night for hordes of women to cascade upon it the next day sent a shiver down Rani's spine. It was unnerving. She was assailed by self-doubt. What was she doing? And Asha and all the other girls and all the customers? Was this place, this fancy room appointed with strange gadgets, really necessary? At this hour, it seemed like part of a strange dream or a figment of a child's imagination.

Women were beautiful, weren't they? So why so much hoo-haa over it? Why the rushed visits, the painstaking makeovers, the painful removal of certain hair and careful grooming of other, and yet the women did go out looking and feeling better. Rani dwelt on this and could come to no conclusion. She threaded Neelam's eyebrows and upper lip at home. Apart from that, Neelam never went to any beauty parlour. Yet Neelam was beautiful, at least she had been until last night when she had lashed out at Papaji.

Rani stood watching out of the window. What was the point, she thought, of this road, or of Jamun Road, of Lawrence Road, of any road? In fact, was there was any point of any of the roads that were laid out all over the world, criss-crossing crazily through towns and cities on the round earth, where groups upon groups of human beings dwelt, full of petty passions and small lives and ambitions and malice. They lived and they died and the next generations carried out the same futile acts.

All dead in the end.

Even the ones with perfectly shaped eyebrows.

At this, Rani's eyes fell on the stove on which they made their tea and the familiar pan and the cups that lay beside it. Suddenly, the topsy-turvy parlour swung back into its right place. Rani thumped her head twice. What had happened to her? She felt a little frightened by herself. She also realized that she was never alone, at home or in the parlour. This was probably the first half hour that she had spent alone ever since she could remember. Is this what solitude was like? There was a loud noise and Rani gave a start. It was just the doorbell. Tremblingly, she made her way to the door and, forgetting all of Asha's security instructions, opened it with a flourish. A man stood there holding a large cardboard box. 'Glow-White Herbal Aids,' he mumbled.

Rani pointed weakly to the reception desk. He hoisted the box full of glowing promises on to the reception desk. Then he whipped out a pen from behind his ear and thrust a piece of paper towards her. Rani signed her name neatly in English.

'Bill?' he asked.

'Asha Madam said she would take care of it,' Rani answered.

The man nodded and asked for a glass of water. Rani handed him one. He took out a strip of aspirin from his pocket, popped one into his mouth and swallowed it. He handed the glass back to

Rani, saying, 'This is the most effective. Never take it on an empty stomach though. A cousin of mine did and she got an ulcer. Three units of blood they had to give her.'

Rani nodded and took the glass back.

The man left.

Relieved, Rani switched off the light, locked up and went home.

Eleven

While walking home, Rani saw Satish's mother standing by the gate of her house as she usually did. As soon as she saw Rani, she exclaimed, 'Oh Rani, don't you know, Dheeraj Bhaisaab fainted today. Right in the middle of the bazaar.'

Rani stopped, not taking it in.

'Where?'

'In front of the fruit stalls. Lucky no scooter or motorcycle was right behind.'

'Is he okay?' Rani asked, her mouth dry, her voice barely a whisper.

'Yes, I think so. I mean, they had to help him up and give him water and take him home.'

'Where is Mahesh?'

'He came back from the mill to see his father. But now both he and Satish are at the shop.'

Rani felt furious with Mahesh. Couldn't he have stayed at home with Papaji?

She quickened her steps towards home. Why would Papaji faint? He had never fainted before. Could it be anything to do with blood pressure? What else? Frustrated, Rani wished she was better informed. When she reached home, Dheeraj was sitting calmly in his usual chair, engrossed in his newspaper. Bittu was drawing leaves on Dheeraj's feet with a new green sketch pen.

'Just draw. Don't tickle,' Dheeraj was telling him mildly as Rani entered.

Rani rushed to Dheeraj, knelt by his chair and hugged his knees.

'Papaji, what happened, Papaji?'

'Nothing, Rani.' Dheeraj said placing a hand on her head. 'What's wrong?'

Rani began to sob, still clutching at her father's knees. The clean, crisp cotton of his pyjamas felt reassuring against her cheek. 'They said you had fainted in the market today.'

'Who said that?'

'Satish's mother did.'

'Just felt a little dizzy and fell. You know the women in this mohalla. Life without drama just doesn't suit their health.'

Bittu's voice piped up from below both of them.

'Dadu, she is spoiling the leaf.'

Rani snapped at him, 'Animal! Go and draw in your drawing book! You are always underfoot.'

Bittu got up and walked away. 'Even if you tried,' he said to Rani scathingly, 'you couldn't draw a peepul leaf half as well as I can.'

Rani ignored him and turned to her father again with an anxious face.

'Papaji, don't try to fool me. Nobody faints just like that. You have never fainted before. How could you feel dizzy, it's not even summer!'

Dheeraj tried to avoid meeting her eyes.

'Relax, Rani,' he said. 'It was nothing. I am getting old, after all. Maybe I should be more careful.'

Rani took his chin in her hands and forced him to make eye contact with her. 'No, tell me. Had you eaten? Were you upset by what happened? Did you sleep last night? Has anyone been saying anything else to you? I am your daughter, Papaji, why can't I know what is in your heart?'

Dheeraj folded his newspaper. 'I don't know,' he answered, his voice very slow and deliberate. 'It is not what anybody says.'

He looked about searchingly as if he was about to say something else and then stopped. 'It is difficult for me to explain,' he said gently. 'It is difficult to put what is in my heart into words and sentences.'

Rani asked worriedly, 'Did you go to the doctor?'

'No,' Dheeraj replied, 'but the boy at Janta Chemists, he took my blood pressure. It was normal. Don't you worry now.'

Rani gave him an exasperated look and got to her feet.

'I am going to bring you a glass of hot milk,' she said.

She washed her hands and went into the kitchen. Neelam was there washing utensils. The two hadn't spoken since the upset last night.

Rani measured out a glass of milk, ground some cinnamon and green cardamom together, added it to the pan and waited for the milk to boil.

Neelam continued to wash and stack utensils in silence. The milk boiled, Rani added sugar to it, strained it into a steel tumbler and placed it on a tray. Neelam eyed her, looked as if she was about to say something, but didn't.

When Rani took the milk to her father, Bittu was standing by him with his drawing book in his hand, challenging him to draw white rice on white paper.

'Um ... I didn't mention it or discuss it with you ...' Dheeraj said to Rani, taking the glass from her, 'I'll be away for twelve days, you know. It is a ten-day meditation course, and two days for the travel.'

Rani felt curious and wanted to ask more, but didn't. This apparently meant a lot to Papaji.

'I've never left you alone before, not since your mother died.'

Dheeraj slowly sipped at the hot milk as he spoke. When he finished it, he said, looking deep into the depths of his steel tumbler, 'Not once. Ever. I hope it is okay.'

'Of course it is okay, Papaji. Dharamsala is supposed to be a beautiful place and if this is what you want, of course it is okay. But you must get something for me. I've heard they sell different kinds of earrings there. Tibetan beads and stuff.'

Dheeraj looked alarmed. 'I don't know anything about earrings,' he said.

Rani patted his arm. 'Never mind, then. You don't have to get me anything. But if you just spot a pair of beautiful, affordable Tibetan earrings, buy them, okay?'

Dheeraj nodded.

'And me?' Bittu said. 'What about me?'

'Do you want earrings?' Dheeraj asked, laughing.

'No, but there must be something you can get. Some toys that Dharamsala boys play with.'

'You needn't get us anything, Papaji,' Rani suddenly said, 'Just be happy. And come back safe.'

'Okay,' Bittu said, considering. 'Then, when you are back, you can treat us to ice cream.'

'Some people,' Rani said to Bittu scathingly, 'don't have souls above their stomachs.'

✧ ✧ ✧

Rani could feel that the atmosphere in their home had changed. It had become permanently strained, charged, as if anything could give way at any moment. Mahesh spent less and less time at home. Dheeraj tried to retain normalcy but his face showed the strain within. Neelam, who had always been given to veiled remarks, would now openly lash out at any of them, remaining morose for the rest of the day, eating listlessly and very little.

Even Bittu, whom the harshest of scoldings and remonstrances could not usually touch, seemed a little wary now. He began to spend more time with Karan next door. Rani wished people would leave her father alone. To her, his seemed a benign existence, threatening to no one, interfering with no one, and she could not understand how he could arouse such resentment and passion in other people.

Whenever she saw Dheeraj's frail face look harassed and vulnerable, the memory of Ravan, unforgiven by the world, his face burning up into a sad shrivel would come back to her, filling her with uneasiness.

✧ ✧ ✧

Along with all this, she could also feel something changing inside her. A stillness was creeping into her. Quietly.

She realized what she hadn't until now – that her life seemed to be a series of cacophonic days. Her mornings began in the middle of the family din. Waking up was hectic business, with Bittu being yelled at, the clattering of pans and pots in the kitchen and visits from the milkman and subziwalla.

She always bathed and dressed in a hurry. The walk to the auto-rickshaw stand meant meandering through yelling hawkers and dodging ringing-bells cyclists. The auto rickshaw she finally boarded would be full of people, with the driver yelling his head off for new passengers each time he halted. The passengers would argue with each other over how much space who was taking up.

When she reached work, Asha would begin to snap instructions as soon as one entered the air-conditioned parlour. And all day the women who came to be beautified talked. Talked incessantly. With each other, to the girls, to their husbands and to their servants over their cellphones. There was no pause, no silence. During tea breaks, the girls chatted amongst themselves, glad of the respite from the continuous demands of the customers. Sometimes, sheer relief made them babble.

And then the whole thing was repeated on the way back from work, the same endless cyclists and rickshaws, vendors and honking autos. Then home again, this time the blaring television adding to all the other noises. When added to the recent constant monologue in her head, the noise was becoming unbearable.

And yet, in some strange way, Rani could sense that she was becoming stiller and quieter inside.

✧ ✧ ✧

The next week, Dheeraj left for Dharamsala. He packed his brown attaché case and, after assuring Rani that he had enough woollens and socks, departed to the bus stand. Mahesh and Neelam saw him off too, silently. Bittu waved till the rickshaw carrying Dheeraj turned the street corner and disappeared from sight.

Twelve

It was the day of the puja ceremony. Bittu squatted by the hired cook, who had set up his oversized cooking utensils in the courtyard. 'Who taught you to cook?' he asked.

'My master,' the cook said. 'I was your age when I became his assistant.'

'Can I become your assistant?' Bittu asked eagerly.

'Go and ask your mother,' the cook answered.

Bittu stuck out his stomach a little in imitation of the cook. It made him feel grand and grown-up to be squatting beside this man of the world, conversing as an equal.

'My mother,' he said loyally, 'is a very nice lady, but she refuses everything before even listening what it is about.'

'Women can be like that,' the cook agreed understandingly.

Bittu was pleased at this.

'What are you going to cook?'

'I'll cook what I have been told to. Puris, chhole, halwa – the usual.'

'How many puris can you eat at one go?' Bittu asked.

Here he was interrupted by Rani, who wanted him in for his bath. Sighing like a martyr, he went indoors. It was a bit of a pose, since he was looking forward to dressing up.

He usually took a bath on his own, but today his mother took over, washing behind his ears and scrubbing the soles of his feet with a pumice stone. Then, dressed just in his underpants, he was delivered to Rani. She helped him dress in a silk kurta-pyjama especially bought for the occasion. Bittu couldn't take his eyes off the mirror.

'When I grow up ...'

Rani interrupted him. 'Yes, yes, I know, you are going to be the biggest hero. Show me your nails now.'

His nails passed inspection and Rani combed his hair neatly.

'Is Seema Bua coming?' He asked.

'Yes she is.'

'Then Karan will come too. I have never seen him in a silk kurta-pyjama.'

'Bittu,' Rani said, 'you are still looking like a monkey. So shut up. And you are not to go out and play now and dirty your clothes. Go and sit with your mother while I get dressed.' Rani pushed him out of the room and changed into a light orange salwar-kameez. It was supposed to be an auspicious colour.

Rani hoped fervently that the shadows over their home would disappear and that an auspicious time would begin for the family.

✧ ✧ ✧

Pandit Dina Nath had everything ready. He had the ceremonial fire going and various utensils that contained the offerings he would put into it. He sat there, looking pious, while guests trickled in, the small house slowly becoming crammed with limbs, voices, scented hair oil and gossip. Savitri and Rakesh from next door had arrived, along with Seema and Karan. Harsh couldn't make it and Chitra came in late, breaking into giggles as soon as she saw Pandit Dina Nath. Savitri gave her a stern look and Chitra sat down decorously.

Other neighbours drifted in, saying polite 'namastes' to each other before settling down.

Then Neelam's corpulent brothers arrived along with their wives, who dripped gold-plated jewellery. Neelam looked proud. This was how a home should be like. With everyone well dressed, prayers taking place and people coming in to bless them. Not a strange, ascetic place where nobody came and went, where there was too much silence, too much contemplation.

She finally felt part of the mainstream – a normal woman with a normal home. She greeted all the guests with folded hands, and bowed and scraped to Pandit Dina Nath, who lapped it all up. She offered him dainties and savouries till he told her in irritation that he could eat only after the havan was completed. There was pleasurable excitement all around. Rani thought that purifying ceremonies in this mohalla were like surprise parties, especially when not many weddings were happening.

The ceremony began. Well-wishers sat respectfully with folded hands. Children, despite maternal warnings, managed to run around the house with a keen eye on the cook's area of work. Seema sat by Rani and muttered in her ear, 'Looking very pretty and all. Is Satish coming?'

Rani ignored her, closing her eyes piously. Then she thought of her father and actually began to pray earnestly. It was the first time she was doing so at a prayer ceremony. Usually she would just sit with her eyes closed, hands folded and let her mind wander pleasurably.

But today, a few heartfelt prayers murmured in despair went up heavenwards.

The chanting was hypnotic; the smells of incense and condiments put into the fire filled the room. The ceremony was concluded in half an hour after which the spiritual atmosphere suddenly exploded, leaving behind cackling laughter, chatter and gossip.

The food was ready. Neelam first offered it to Pandit Dina Nath along with a gift of clothes and money and then began to persuade her guests, urging them to eat. Rani began to get bored.

'Let's find a corner and sit down,' she said to Seema.

About twenty red plastic chairs had been hired for the occasion. The girls dragged two of these to the corner of the courtyard and settled down with their plates.

'My grandmother has gone crazy,' Seema said. 'All she talks of is the urgent need to get me married off to a suitable boy.'

'So get married,' Rani said facetiously. 'You can have a good time harassing your mother-in-law – that should suit you.'

The two giggled. Then a squat woman dressed in a loud purple sari who was standing at the opposite end of the courtyard, her plate loaded with halwa, asked Rani in a voice that was as loud as her sari. 'Where is your father, Rani?'

A few people fell silent, waiting for the reply. Rani said, 'Oh, he has gone to ...'

Neelam, who was carrying a tray containing tumblers of tea, hastily interrupted, in an unnaturally loud voice, 'Papaji had to go for some urgent work. He really wanted to be here today but couldn't.'

'It is very important for the family elders to be present at such functions,' Purple Sari said lugubriously. One of Neelam's brothers nodded gravely.

'Yes, but what can be done. There are other duties,' Neelam said, blushing.

Rakesh said, 'I heard Bittu say to Karan that his grandfather was off to Dharamsala.'

Neelam looked nonplussed. Then she recovered. 'You know Bittu. Tomorrow he will say his grandfather has gone to the moon.'

Rakesh laughed. 'We wouldn't be surprised even by that,' he said, a trace of nastiness in his jovial voice. 'Why, I even saw him talking to the beggars outside Durgiana Mandir. And he was eating with them.'

Another man piped up, 'And once I saw him teaching some urchins the Hindi alphabet under the banyan tree behind the government school. Very good intentions, but I don't know. My nephew, you know the one who just got married, he is a driver. He takes his employer's daughter to Sacred Heart School for girls. Now he was telling me that while he was waiting for her after school one day, what does he see? He sees Dheeraj Bhaisaab coming out of the school chapel. Must have been praying! Nothing wrong with it but my nephew was just very puzzled. I mean, well, I suppose sometimes people do strange things as they get older.'

Everyone was listening now. Some looked curious, others merely mystified. Then Neelam's brother asked in a slightly shocked voice, loud enough for everyone to hear, 'What does he do? What is he up to, that all these people talk of him? We thought we were marrying you into a good Hindu household.'

Rakesh vigorously nodded his head in agreement. Rani could have slapped him.

Rani seethed with anger. She got to her feet and said, 'Papaji is a very good man. He is actually ... what one is supposed to be.' Here she faltered. 'No need to say anything about Papaji.'

Neelam's brother looked offended. So did Rakesh. He said huffily, 'I only asked because we treat this like our own family. Otherwise, what is it to us? People can go where they want, sit and eat with dirty half-castes, worship strange religions. Though to us Lord Ram is good enough but maybe he is not for some people. We don't mind. We just speak when we consider someone our own. But if we are considered outsiders, why should we bother?' He was working himself up into a fine rhetoric.

Neelam looked close to tears. She went up to Rakesh, 'Don't say that, Bhaisaab. You are like my elder brother. Rani is just a child, even though she is old enough to know better.'

When Rakesh didn't reply, she said, wiping away a tear, 'What can I do of my fate? Even on an auspicious day there is unpleasantness. Is it my fault that our elders behave the way they do?'

Hearing her blame her fate, Rakesh was mollified. 'Don't cry, sister. We are all here for you,' he said, waving his arm around the horribly crammed courtyard.

'God will surely bless a house where the lady is so pious.'

Everyone seemed happy now. Seema, Rakesh's daughter and Rani's best friend, looked a little ashamed and wouldn't meet Rani's eyes. Rani felt furious, disloyal to Papaji. She should have stood up for him better, more strongly.

Bittu came up to her. 'How many raisins did you get in your portion of halwa?' he asked her.

Rani could not answer. She blindly made her way through the crowd, left the gathering behind her and went indoors, where some children were playing and a woman sat with her baby suckling at her breast. Rani wished, for the first time in her life, that she had a room of her own. She remembered the half hour spent alone at Eve's Beauty Parlour and wondered if solitude made you a different person, made you see and live differently. Did you need big rooms to have big souls?

She went into the kitchen where three women stood, discussing the suicide of some woman with relish. Rani wandered disconsolately till everyone had finally gone home. Leftovers had been given away to children, the cook had packed up his paraphernalia and left. Neelam rested in her room and even Bittu, his stomach distended under his silk kurta, lay fast asleep.

Rani changed into her home clothes and lay down, still hearing incessant chatter in her ears. She opened *Filmfare*. Soon, she was engrossed in the cover story that was about the rivalry between two top heroines. She skipped over difficult words and slang. Soon, she had forgotten all else and there was peace.

✧ ✧ ✧

Dheeraj returned after ten days. He seemed thinner, yet his eyes were radiant, his face fresh. He hugged Rani and Bittu, patted Mahesh on the back. Neelam touched his feet and he blessed her affectionately. Rani was overjoyed that he looked better. She had many questions for him but decided she would wait a little.

That evening when they all sat down to eat, Neelam said awkwardly, 'Papaji, I hope you have nothing in your heart against me. I have my own worries. What I said wasn't the way it sounds ...'

Dheeraj interrupted her with a smile. 'The day you came into this house as a young bride,' he told her gently, 'I accepted you as a second daughter. And a daughter has a right to be angry with her father. I make mistakes, like all humans. Let it go.'

More than his words, it was his smile that convinced Neelam that all was forgiven. She felt relieved. Now there would be peace in the home even if for just a while. The ceremony conducted by Pandit Dina Nath had worked then, she thought triumphantly.

Thirteen

A few days passed in peace. Dheeraj appeared to be in good spirits and his movements seemed brisker. And then Rani noticed signs of restlessness in him again. He once again took to staying away from the house for long hours, not coming in at mealtimes, poring over books and staring out the window endlessly. His face became gaunt and strained again and Rani became apprehensive.

One evening, Rani and Dheeraj were alone at home together. This was a rare occurrence. A friend of Mahesh's was getting married and though all of them had been invited, Rani and Dheeraj had opted to stay back. Neelam, Mahesh and Bittu, bathed and dressed in their finery, had gone by themselves. Rani and Dheeraj sat in the main room in peaceful silence. Dheeraj sat in his chair with his eyes closed though Rani knew that he wasn't asleep. Rani sat on the floor painting her nails with a new bottle of shimmery mauve paint.

The silence was beautiful.

Rani finished painting her nails and then leaned back against the wall, stretching out her hands and feet, waiting for the paint to dry.

Her glance fell on Dheeraj's face. It looked vulnerable in repose. Rani sat looking at him and thinking for several minutes. Then she broke the silence.

' Papaji,' she said.

'Hm?'

'Is everything alright?'

'Yes?' he said, sounding surprised, opening his eyes.

'No, I mean, why have things been a little strange?'

Dheeraj opened his eyes and turned his head to look at her. Then he turned away.

'Papaji, please talk to me. Is something troubling you?' Rani said, feeling frustrated at not being able to word her questions aptly.

Dheeraj remained silent.

'All things cannot be answered and explained,' he said, finally meeting her eyes.

'But why do I get this feeling that people find you strange? That you are not happy? Why do you wander the streets? What am I missing?'

Dheeraj looked at the oval face of her daughter with the bright, shining eyes and the earnest expression. She was so like her mother.

'I don't know myself,' he said. 'It is just that the older I grow, the less I know. The more I want to seek.'

'Seek what?'

Dheeraj looked at her helplessly. 'I don't know. I really don't. I wish I did.'

They sat in silence for a while, Rani trying to understand what her father meant. But before she could frame her next question, he said softly, almost as if he were talking to himself, 'Time passes by so quickly. When you are young, you think something will happen – some event or circumstance – that will lead you to a larger meaning. It is as if you are always waiting for that something which is just around the corner. But then you keep turning corners and more corners and you realize you will never know. Never know where you were headed, or if you were headed anywhere at all. The gurus, the teachers, the wise men, the books – you keep following them, hoping against hope that some glimmer of light will shine through. I don't know, at times I feel I might be going insane. At other times, when I am standing in the middle of the tangled lives of people, I feel I am the only sane person I know. And after your mother died … it seemed time did not matter, that life was just a dream, or a joke, and would be over before you knew it. And that everything we do passes away with that moment, leaving no imprint.'

Dheeraj took a sip of water from the glass by his side. 'I am talking nonsense, am I not? I know. It scares me, feeling like this all the time. But I feel it even if I try to deny it.' Then, disconnectedly, he added, 'I don't even know whether I have been a good father, I don't know if any act or any words of mine have had any value.'

Dheeraj smiled at Rani. 'And so these are the rantings of your old father. No wonder you prefer to read about that silly fellow with untidy hair.'

'Shahrukh Khan,' Rani replied in an absent-minded voice.

Dheeraj leaned back and closed his eyes again. He began to softly hum an old song. Rani's nails were dry now but they did not please her as they should have. She still hadn't comprehended the demons her father seemed to be fighting in solitariness.

The feeling of being lost began to grow inside her.

✧ ✧ ✧

The next morning Asha was in one of her moods again. More bills had arrived and a hairdryer had stopped working. All the girls were trying to blame each other for it.

To make matters worse, the first customer was a haughty woman who complained about every single thing. The girls held the dryer too close to her head. Now they held it too far away. The bleach was made too strong. Didn't they know her skin was delicate? The massage that followed the pedicure gave her no relief. They were all inefficient. Though this woman left after paying a hefty bill, she also left behind headaches and bad temper.

Asha looked tired and was impatient with the smallest mistake.

Kavita, who had been told to boil water, let it all boil away.

'You girls are so silly,' Asha shouted at her. 'Here I am paying for the gas, making economies everyday and you let all the water boil away. Get your mind off your stupid wedding and concentrate.'

At this, Kavita went into the alcove and cried for a good ten minutes till Navpreet consoled her with a cup of tea. But Asha seemed unapologetic.

'Oh yes,' she said. 'You girls are the only ones who have emotions and hearts. I am just supposed to be this machine who has to keep you happy, the customers happy, the bills paid and the parlour running.'

Asha went up to the reception desk and thrust the Laughing Buddha into Rani's hands, who was standing close by. 'Take this. It has been of no good to me.'

Rani took it wordlessly. Not knowing what to do with it, she put it in the pocket of her apron, where she usually put combs and tweezers.

After this outburst, Asha dissolved into tears and Navpreet briskly produced another consoling cup of tea.

Shama, who at lunchtime had been overcome by gluttony, had eaten oily pav-bhaji at the filthiest stall in the neighbourhood. She spent the late afternoon puking into the sink when she should have been filing nails into perfect crescents. Asha and the girls spoke loudly to the customers and clattered the drawers unnecessarily to drown out the noises of the by now slimy pav-bhaji being ejected forcefully into the sink.

Asha sprinkled jasmine room freshener liberally in the parlour, in case the stench of the vomit wafted through into the lovely atmosphere of creamed, massaged and perfumed beauties. Later, Asha scolded Shama soundly. 'The more I try,' she said, 'to turn all of you into polished, refined girls, the more idiotic and brainless you get.' Shama ignored her completely, covering her face with a damp hand towel and leaning back in a chair like a masked martyr. At the end of the tiring day, Asha said, 'Girls, you have to get serious. December and January is the wedding season. All the auspicious dates fall within these two months. There will be a lot of work – brides, bridegroom's sisters, their friends and cousins – but only if we run this place like a dream. There is a lot of competition. There is that new Bliss Beauty Parlour that has opened right on the next block. If they pull our customers away in this wedding season, we will never get them back.' The girls nodded wearily. Before leaving, Rani absently transferred the Laughing Buddha from her apron to her purse. There was very little chatter that day. Shama was given a slice of lemon to suck on on her way home and then everybody left, leaving the ghost of the beauty parlour alone for the night.

✧ ✧ ✧

That night, not knowing what else to do with it, Rani handed the little Laughing Buddha to her father. He smiled lovingly and placed it with all the other idols on his shelf.

Fourteen

November passed bleakly. After his brief burst of confidence in Rani, Dheeraj had withdrawn into a shell again, speaking little. He would leave home after just one dry rusk and a cup of tea and stay out most of the day, occasionally just buying a banana or two from a fruit stall. And at dinner, he would have just one roti or very little rice, with a few spoonfuls of dal or vegetables. It worried Rani, and she tried to persuade him to take better care of his health but he had become inaccessible. He would listen to everyone peacefully, and then go about his own way. Soon, they were forced to leave him alone.

It was in the last week of November when Neelam's brother called to say that his wife had delivered a baby boy. It was a happy occasion – they had been married ten years. Neelam was excited and bought clothes for the newborn and fruit for the new mother. Even Dheeraj seemed slightly cheered and went out, to return in half an hour, holding an absurdly large Amritsar version of Winnie the Pooh. The whole family got dressed to go and see the baby who had been delivered in Amritsar Government Hospital. They hired two cycle rickshaws. Neelam and Mahesh got onto one, laden with clothes and fruit. Dheeraj and Rani got onto the other, Bittu and the Amritsari Winnie the Pooh squeezed between them.

Neelam was delighted to see her nephew. Bittu was enchanted, though a little suspicious. He looked at the wrinkled red face and asked, 'Where did he come from?'

The proud, tired mother answered from her bed, 'I was asleep and God came and left him here.'

Bittu whispered to Rani, 'She is lying. I know they live in the mothers' stomachs. Doesn't it bother them when food falls on their heads, bits of roti and pickle and all? And imagine when the mothers eat curd. It must have come pouring down on his head, cold and wet. How did he come out? Did she vomit him out?'

Rani grimaced and shut him up.

Dheeraj held the baby and blessed him. 'I remember when Mahesh was born,' he said with a rare, happy smile. The family spent a pleasurable hour with the baby and the many relatives milling around.

When the new mother needed to feed the baby, Neelam stayed inside. Dheeraj and Rani discreetly left the room and sat outside on a hard wooden bench.

They heard Neelam crooning over the baby. 'Thank God,' Dheeraj and Rani heard her say, 'that He has finally blessed you with such a fine boy. Protect him from the evil eye.'

The mother sighed. 'Thanks to Lord Krishna, he has sent a spitting image of himself. Now I can be at peace. Years and years, tests after tests, and all girls. My body is tired after all those abortions.'

'Never mind,' Neelam said consolingly. 'Think of the baby as your reward for all your sufferings.'

The two began to croon over the baby again.

Dheeraj and Rani sat dumbly, too stunned even to look at each other.

And an unsaid, unspoken thought floated between them. Bittu was an only child ... conceived after four years of marriage ... Had Neelam ...?

When they went back into the room, the Amritsar Winnie the Pooh appeared to stare at them malevolently, a sullen monster. Rani saw that Dheeraj's hands were trembling.

✧ ✧ ✧

Finally, late in the evening, they left the hospital. Rani made Bittu wear his woollen cap and muffler and drew her shawl close over his head. Bittu nodded sleepily all the way home, snuggling into her side like a puppy.

When Mahesh was unlocking the front door of their house in the semi-dark, he heard a squelching sound under his rubber slippers. The front step was wet. Confused, he unlocked the door and pushed it open. Dismayed, he looked around. The rest of the family nudged him aside to peer into the house. Neelam went pale.

The main room was flooded. The water was knee-deep. Rani and Bittu's mattresses were soaked. So were the mats on which they sat to have their meals. 'What is this?' Neelam whispered. She took off her chappals, hitched up her sari and, with her cracked heels and silver anklets showing, waded into the room. Everyone else followed in silence.

The ancient water tank, the old pipes and the weary, unrepaired walls that had withheld the onslaught of many monsoons had now given way in the middle of the dry, cold winter. The source of the pipe burst was in the kitchen. The drains had not been able to take the volume of water that gushed forth from the burst pipe and the neighbourhood sewage system was poor. The drains of the house had been driven to their limit and had firmly closed up. In the hours they had been away, the water had made its way from the kitchen to the rest of the small house, covering every square inch of the floor. Then the level had gone up, soaking, crumbling and dissolving whatever it could.

The old house had finally given up its effort to exist.

Neelam wordlessly made her way to the kitchen and cursed herself for not having emptied the new sack of flour into the big brass drum. Twenty kilos of good wheat flour, that was meant to last them for at least two months, lay there soaked. Steel utensils floated gloomily.

Dheeraj went to his room or, rather, the curtained-off space he called his room. His shelf of idols was untouched, but the books that he had neatly stacked by his bed were ruined, their pages sticking to each other, the print running off some of the cheaper ones.

Bittu's school bag seemed to have lain in water for hours. His books, exercise notebooks and new World Atlas were all beyond repair. A copy of *Filmfare* floated face up. A warped Kareena Kapoor smiled from its cover, staring at the ceiling fan pointlessly.

Mahesh stood alone, looking around him, perplexed. The house looked like a shot from the TV footage of the floods that happened in some village or the other ever year in India. Mahesh went from room to room, turning off every electric switch with Bittu's wooden ruler so that there would be no chances of short circuiting and electrocution.

Nobody spoke a word till Neelam went into her room to check the damage there. The water had got into the in-built cupboard. On the lowest shelf had lain Neelam's wedding sari, carefully wrapped in tissue paper. The paper had disintegrated, the sari with delicate zari work that had cost so much then, and the design of which Neelam had chosen after three days' deliberation, till her mother had threatened to kill herself unless she made a quick decision, now lay in ruins. It was as if the sight of the ruined sari broke something deep inside Neelam. She began to wail as if she was mourning someone's death.

✧ ✧ ✧

It was to be a strange night for the family. Bittu had been unaffected, in fact a little delighted at the flooding, till he discovered that all his favourite kites and comics had been attacked by the cruel, insidious water. He cried then, quite inconsolably, till Dheeraj promised to get him new kites and Rani swore to him that she would try and find the exact comics even if she had to scour through Hall Bazaar for them. Neelam, her fit of wailing over, was walking around, looking almost crazy, picking up things at random and then discarding them. The night grew colder outside and there was no warm corner in the house. The bed in Neelam's room was dry. Rani covered it with a blanket and put Bittu on it. She wondered how long it would take to wade into the kitchen, locate a pan and a glass, the milk in the fridge and make a hot drink for Bittu. And what about Papaji? Where would he sleep?

Worried, Rani went up to Mahesh and Neelam and said, 'It is

only nine o'clock. They'll still be up next door. I will go and talk to Seema. Maybe Bittu and Papaji can sleep in their house and someone can come and help clear this up.'

She anxiously turned to Mahesh, 'Do you think you can get hold of a plumber at this hour? Even if this is a job for the municipal corporation, we still need someone to fix this meanwhile.' Neelam suddenly snapped at Rani, 'You keep quiet. You are not the head of the house.' Here, she shot an accusing look at Dheeraj. 'These decisions are for your brother to take. All you need to do is just do as you are told.' Rani shrank back, hurt in her eyes.

'Nobody is sleeping over at any neighbours',' Neelam continued vehemently. 'I don't want the whole mohalla to be laughing at us tomorrow. Everyone except us in this mohalla gets their houses whitewashed every year. If they are poor they do it themselves, but they do it. And repairs happen along with whitewash. Nobody but us live in a house with cracked walls. Even the washerwoman had a new tin roof put up this monsoon. No. If we live here, then we will spend our nights here. If I hear one more taunt from anybody, I'll die. Enough is enough.'

Mahesh protested. 'But it is night-time,' he said. 'If we start cleaning up now, people can see anyway. You are being unreasonable. At least let the child go.'

But Neelam was adamant. She locked the front door and said, 'Now nobody can see us. We'll manage alone.'

Dheeraj stood silently all this while, a faint look of helpless humiliation on his face.

Mahesh sighed wearily. 'It never ends. Always running around, working in the mill, standing in queues for something or the other or cycling around this blasted city.'

Neelam didn't respond.

Then he said more calmly, 'The shops will all be closed. But I think I know where a plumber called Raju lives. I will go to his home.' He slipped out, wheeled his bicycle out of the courtyard and disappeared into the cold, foggy night.

✧ ✧ ✧

The night was a long and weary one. Rani managed to give Bittu a hot glass of milk, and tucked him up in the sole dry blanket in Neelam's bed where he finally slept. She put a pillow each on either side of Bittu. She was afraid that, unused to sleeping on a bed, he might roll off and land in the water below. Neelam had not spoken a word to Dheeraj or looked at him ever since they had entered the house. He was expecting what would come his way later. But for now, he concentrated on trying to get the kitchen drain unblocked. Rani and Neelam did not know where to begin. They took the largest tumblers from the kitchen, brought two buckets in from the tiny bathroom and began the long task of scooping water from the floor into the buckets. Once a bucket was full, they'd take it to the tiny toilet and pour it down the flush, hoping that in that area at least, some mysterious, miraculous drain would still be open.

Dheeraj's white pyjamas were by now filthy up to the knees with the scum that he was scooping out of the drain. He ignored the stench and finally managed to unblock the drain partially. A couple of hours passed before Mahesh came back with a sleepy-eyed man, Raju, the plumber. He looked around the house glumly, then, with resigned eyes, opened his toolbox.

✧ ✧ ✧

The next day was chaotic. Rani called up Asha from the corner PCO and pleaded for a day off. She gave Asha the real reason, not caring how it sounded, and Asha agreed. Two plumbers from the municipal corporation came over, three workers were employed. The urgent repairs were done, a black Sintex water tank sat shinily on the roof beside the old stone tank which the plumbers declared not fit to be used any longer. The floors were still wet, the workers left muddy footprints everywhere. Mattresses and mats were put in the courtyard to dry.

'A slight accident,' Neelam explained with a rueful smile to any passer-by who happened to ask.

Bittu had refused to go to school. 'Even if I die,' he explained earnestly to Rani, 'Tripathi Sir will expect my corpse to have the atlas.' Tripathi Sir was Bittu's geography teacher. He also taught history and social science. By the afternoon, Rani was exhausted. Dheeraj and Mahesh had been going up and down with the workers continuously. Neelam and Rani had supplied cups of tea and dry rusks. That was all they could manage. At two, Rani went to a food stall nearby and, out of her own money, bought enough aloo-puri to feed everyone in the house. After lunch, exhausted, Rani asked Neelam if she could now take Bittu next door. Neelam agreed and herself sat down to rest on the wooden bench in the kitchen.

Rani was relieved to find that Seema and her grandmother were alone in the house.

The grandmother, whom everyone called 'Beeji', peered at Rani.

'Not gone to your beauty parlour today?' she asked.

'No.' Rani smiled brightly at her. 'Why work everyday?'

Beeji smiled. 'As young girls,' she said, 'we used to work *all* the time.' Here she paused and her cataracted eyes gazed into some vague space. 'But that was before Partition,' she finished, and went to sit in the verandah to doze.

Rani told Seema what had happened, also instructing her not to mention it to anyone.

'Bhabhi is touchy about it,' she explained.

Seema nodded. 'My bhabhis are also half mad,' she said understandingly.

Bittu was disappointed that Karan wasn't home. Then he parked himself in front of the TV.

Finally, Rani let herself relax. She bathed and dressed in a salwar-kameez borrowed from Seema. She ate dal and rice and so did Bittu. After lunch, all three of them napped. At about four in the evening, word was sent to Rani and Bittu that the work was finished and they could return.

'Have a cup of tea before you leave,' Seema said. Rani knew there would be a lot of scrubbing and cleaning to do once she got home and no rest for quite a while so she agreed to stop. After tea, the two went back home. The walls were repaired and patchy, the pipes had been replaced, the workers and plumbers had left. The house was dry, but dirty. When they entered, Dheeraj was standing in the middle of the room, his head hanging in shame. Neelam was in tears. Mahesh was shouting at Dheeraj, the first time Rani had ever heard him do so. 'I spend every rupee I have on household expenses, you know that. You know how difficult things are. And yet you lend all your savings to that good-for-nothing Aman! Are you blind to your own son's plight? And now you say we can't get the money back? That he lied? That he took the money and went off to Jalandhar? And you didn't know?'

Mahesh was in a rage. His eyes were bloodshot, his usually pallid face red. Rani had never felt the horror before that she felt now when she saw her father crying silent tears.

Rani spoke up timidly, 'But what about the money I contribute, Bhaiya? Can that not help?'

Neelam said sharply, 'You also eat, buy clothes and earrings.'

Rani moved closer to her father, resisting the urge to slap her brother.

Mahesh turned and thumped his fist on the wall. 'I don't believe this. The Sintex water tank alone cost ₹1350. Then I have to pay thousands to the plumbers, masons and painters who came to patch the wall up, repair the cracks and paint the wall. The whole month's rations had just been delivered. They were still lying on the kitchen floor. It is completely useless now. I have to pay everyone by this evening. The drain cleaners will have to be called in again. And there have been power cuts at the mill. You know we get paid nothing when there are power cuts. At the most I can stretch it to tomorrow. Plus everything that was ruined by the water has to be replaced. What am I going to do?'

Mahesh was unrecognizable, his face suffused with blood and rage, his voice harsh.

'I have nightmares,' Mahesh said, 'of Bittu spending his life in an airless, lightless factory, working power looms. I want to have enough to educate him. And this is how we are going about it?'

At this, Dheeraj pursed his lips to stop himself from breaking down completely.

Neelam stood silent but there was open anger and accusation on her face. Rani rushed to her father and put her arm around his frail shoulders. 'Stop, Bhaiya. Please stop. This is our Papaji you are talking to. We'll manage. We'll do something.'

Bittu, puzzled, began to cry.

'What are *you* crying for?' Mahesh shouted at him.

He turned to Neelam savagely, 'Shut that kid up right now before I hit him.' Neelam took Bittu's hand and tried to take him out of the room.

Bittu resisted and tried to reach out to Rani instead.

'What is this family coming to?' Neelam said to Rani, 'You have made the child forget who his mother is.' She let go of Bittu's elbow abruptly. 'Go. Go to them. You have also become one of them.'

Rani stood silently by her father's side, tears now running down her own face as well.

The world had turned topsy-turvy.

Fifteen

'Is my bindi dead centre?' the nervous bride asked. Asha reassured her it was. 'Are my lips a nice shape?' Rani assured her wearily that they were.

Rani, for the past few days, had been able to sleep very little. She felt nauseous and nervy most of the time.

The bride's mother, who stood behind her chair, said, 'You are the most beautiful bride in the world, darling,' and became misty-eyed.

'That is not the point, Ma,' the bride snapped back. 'The eyeshadow should look good in real life and in photographs and in the video. Will it?' she turned beseechingly to Asha.

'Of course it will,' Asha said sweetly. 'You are looking just perfect.'

Asha stole a glance at the wall clock. Another bride was due in fifteen minutes.

Eve's Beauty Parlour offered 'bridal packages' spread over five days, beginning with beauty treatments and culminating in the final finished bride. Any customer who came to enquire about the bridal package was given a charming smile by Asha and handed a brochure that she had designed herself. She had debated for two days whether she should have two hearts and a bride on the front cover but then had decided that that was not classy enough. The present brochure cover had a pencil sketch of a beautiful bride and a border of henna designs. Asha was very proud of this brochure.

On the first page it said, 'At Eve's we don't just make you look good, we make you feel good.'

There were just another three pages listing the three packages that they offered, worded thus:

Economy Bridal Package: ₹2,500/-
Manicure + Pedicure + Threading + 2 Facials + Face Bleach + Neck Bleach + Shoulder Bleach + Full Arms, Under Arms and Full Legs Waxing + Head Massage + Shampoo + Water Proof Bridal Makeup + Wedding Hairstyle

Deluxe Bridal Package: ₹4,000/-
Manicure + European Pedicure + Threading + Full Body Wax + Full Body Bleach + Body Massage + 2 Facials + Hot Oil Treatment + Head Massage + Shampoo + Bridal Water Proof Makeup + Wedding Hairstyle + Delicious Lunch

Super Deluxe Bridal Package: ₹5,000/-
Deluxe Manicure + European Pedicure + Threading + Full Body Wax + Full Body Imported Bleach + Full Body Turkish or Holistic Massage + Hot Oil Aromatic Treatment + 1 Facial + 1 Gold or Holistic Facial + Bridal Water Proof and Special Effects Makeup + Wedding Hairstyle + Stress Reduction Therapy + Delicious Lunch

The Stress Reduction Therapy in the last package had been Asha's brainwave. She had read about it in the interview of a famous beautician in *Savvy*. As far as Asha could make out, it meant massages with some aromatherapy oils and deep-breathing exercises. A little flummoxed, Asha had converted this into a massage with lavender oil accompanied by a soothing murmur of good advice and reassurance. To assuage her conscience, she just charged them for the actual lavender oil used.

✧ ✧ ✧

The other bride arrived soon. She was still on her third day of the package. Rani, the crease in her brow almost permanent now, began to warm olive oil for the head massage. Ever since the day the water pipes had burst, Dheeraj had gone from bad to worse.

He even seemed to have lost the will to go out much. He would sit around at home trying not to meet Neelam's eye. He hadn't smiled once, not even when Bittu would play or talk to him. The days had become too heavy for Rani to bear. When the olive oil was warmed, she combed the second bride's hair and began to rub the oil into her scalp in soothing circular motions. She continued for half an hour, her own head aching. No matter what, Mahesh shouldn't have spoken like that to Papaji. How *could* he?

Other regular customers sat around, one deeply engrossed in *Woman's Era* while Kavita filed her nails. Another stood bravely like the Colossus, getting her legs waxed. There was another customer who often came in looking exhausted. She would always ask only for a head massage, never anything else. She was a bit of mystery to the girls and they liked to make wild speculations about her.

The radio played a song:

Duniya banane wale,
Kya tere man mein samaayi?
Kahe ko duniya banaayi ...

✧ ✧ ✧

Rani trudged home wearily at the end of the day. She no longer looked at the earrings stalls or bothered to glance into Satish Electricals to see if Satish was there. She just stopped at a fruit stall to buy some bananas, hoping to coax Papaji into eating one. Or two, if she was lucky. Bittu wasn't home when she got there. He had sensed the change at home and spent a lot of his evenings playing with Karan next door. Neelam was taking some laundry off the clothesline in the courtyard. Rani said a quiet namaste to her and she nodded back. That was all the interaction they had these days. Rani went in and did not find Dheeraj sitting in his chair. She went to his bed and saw him lying there, beads of perspiration on his forehead. She bent down by his side and wiped it off with the end of her chunni.

'Papaji, are you unwell?'

'No,' he said.

Rani could have screamed in frustration. She kept her voice calm and asked again, 'You are perspiring, yet it is freezing outside. Are you in pain?'

'A little bit,' he answered.

'Where?'

'Generally. All over. And in my left arm. I'll sleep for a while. Can you get me some water?'

Rani saw that the earthen pot out of which Dheeraj drank was empty. Too fatigued to be angry, Rani went to the kitchen, washed the pot and refilled it. Though they had a refrigerator, Dheeraj always drank water out of an earthen pot, the way he had since his childhood.

Rani fetched the filled pot back and a freshly washed steel tumbler. Dheeraj sat up with some difficulty, took some tablets out of a pouch on his bedside table and washed down two with water.

'What is that medicine, Papaji?'

'Nothing much. For pain.'

'Do you need to see a doctor?' she asked.

Dheeraj looked at her and patted her head in his usual gesture. 'No, Rani. Let me sleep now.'

'Have you eaten? Will you have a banana?'

'Tomorrow,' he said, his eyes unfocused. He turned his back towards her, drawing up his quilt.

Rani stood there helplessly. She noticed that the little idols and pictures on the shelf above were dusty.

✧ ✧ ✧

The second bride's wedding day also arrived. Another lehnga, another set of jewellery, another make-up session, some vanity, some hysterics and another bride was ready to live through a marriage. She was only the second to have taken a bridal package this year and Rani was already becoming sick of brides. Kavita's wedding date had been finalized too. It was to be on 6 April, an auspicious day for them according to their pandit. Kavita shyly asked Asha if she could get any help to get ready on her wedding day. Asha was indignant.

'Help, what do you mean help? One of our girls is getting married. All these other good-for-nothings will help you. And I will do your hair and make-up with my own hands.' Kavita and Asha exchanged their first sentimental glance in the four years they had worked together.

'What are you wearing?' Dolly asked Kavita.

'A red salwar-kameez,' Kavita answered glumly. 'My mother refused to let me wear an Anarkali kurta on my wedding day. But she did agree to let me get two stitched finally to wear later as a new bride. I will give all of you invitation cards as soon as they are printed,' she said smilingly. 'My brother's friend is a printer so we are getting a forty per cent discount. You must all come with your families.'

Kavita, who was slightly bucktoothed with an elongated face, was actually looking beautiful with that smile. Rani impetuously ran to her and gave her a hug. Everyone looked vaguely embarrassed and happy. After a pause, Shama said thoughtfully, 'What does forty per cent exactly mean? What does per cent mean? I have always wondered.'

Asha gave her a hard look and she came back to herself. 'Off to work now, all of you.' Asha said briskly. And the girls dispersed.

Sixteen

'Rani Bua, it is 31st December today,' Bittu said. 'What New Year present are you giving me?'

'Have you ever even heard of anyone getting New Year presents?'

'Okay, don't,' Bittu said. 'I thought no harm in trying.'

'And don't start troubling your grandfather about presents either. Okay?'

'I won't,' Bittu answered in a quiet voice, turning his head away from Rani.

Bittu was troubled about his grandfather but did not know what to think, what to ask.

It was best to stay silent about it, he had decided.

Rani saw his face change and realized how neglected he had been. She put an arm around Bittu.

'Tonight there will be many New Year programmes on TV. Let us get some nice things to eat and we can have a good time.' Bittu visibly cheered up.

'And we can ask Dadu too?' he asked.

'Yes, we can,' Rani said, suddenly feeling hopeful.

But when they went to ask Dheeraj, he was lying in bed, the pallor on his face frightening, his eyes vacantly staring at the ceiling.

Rani felt immense grief at the sight. She did not know how the calm, principled and affectionate man had come to this point in his journey. The clean, quiet corner of the home which had once housed her father's few books, a Hanuman Chalisa and the pictures of a few gods on a battered tin trunk was now changed. He lay on his charpai all day long, his bedside table crowded with bottles and jars – cough syrup, tiger balm, eye-drops, hot water bottle and pain-relief tablets.

'Papaji,' she said. 'It is New Year's Eve tonight. There will be special TV programmes. Will you watch them with us? Please.'

Bittu held Dheeraj's clammy hand. 'Please Dadu, please, please. Dadu, please. We can eat too. Ma never scolds or refuses anything on New Year's Eve.' Then he added magnanimously, 'And you can choose the food. We will get only that. Samosas, cotton candy, chips, tikkis with chutney, chowmein from Jagdamba Chinese Stall, anything. You name it. I will get it all.'

'I have a whole fifty rupees saved,' he boasted. 'The money you gave me on Diwali,' he added sheepishly.

Dheeraj smiled at the two eager, worried faces. 'All the good and the bad we do comes back to us,' he said. 'And you two have definitely resulted from something very good I must have done, sometime, somewhere.' After this lucid sentence, his attention seemed to wander again. When the two repeated their entreaties, he said, 'No. I am too tired. You two enjoy yourselves.'

Bittu looked disappointed and Rani immediately took his hand. 'Never mind, monkey. Grandfather can celebrate with us next year. He might enjoy your company better then too. Hopefully in one year you will grow some brains. Let's go and buy goodies.'

The two went out and had a lovely evening. They bought two plates of chowmein from Jagdamba Chinese Stall. And as a rare treat, a one-litre bottle of Pepsi which he usually had only on Diwali. Then they bought two samosas and two small pineapple pastries each. Bittu demanded extra chutney for the samosas and interrogated the shopkeeper at great length about the freshness of the pastries. The shopkeeper called him a scoundrel but with a smile. Then, for good measure, they bought large bags of potato chips from a man who fried them fresh at a stall every evening.

'Is this enough?' Bittu asked Rani anxiously.

'Quite enough,' Rani said firmly. 'Even for New Year's Eve.'

'We'll have the pastries at the end,' Bittu said, meticulously planning the feast in his head.

Laden with their precious, aromatic bags, they returned. It was only eight and Rani was surprised to find Dheeraj already asleep. Neelam and Mahesh were having their dinner, anticipating that the other two would wait up for the strange middle-of-the-night television feast. They talked desultorily for a while. Then Neelam went to bed and Mahesh went out for a last after-dinner beedi with Satish.

With anticipatory bliss, Rani and Bittu settled down in front of the television. They placed their now-dried-to-death mattresses comfortably, piled all the cushions and pillows around to make comfortable bolsters for themselves and, with the first drink of Pepsi in their hands, switched on the television. Bittu hadn't felt this happy for ages. Neither had Rani. It was like the old times. They avidly watched all the advertisements, commenting on each one of them. While Rani was extremely skeptical that women had actually washed half of their faces with Dove while carefully washing the other half with another brand of soap and had found the Dove side softer, as the advertisement claimed, Bittu wasn't. In fact, he felt it was more interesting to wash your face in halves or, better still, in quarters. They giggled and giggled at this.

At the next advertisement, Bittu immediately vowed to give up all the boring food cooked in his house and have Maggi noodles everyday, the kind that the cheerful mother in the ad was enthusiastically serving her child. Bittu noted that the fresh-faced, smiling Maggi Mother did not once complain that she was tired or that Maggi was expensive and useless, that cooking gas was expensive, that she could not cook different things for different family members and that her son was a scamp.

The two flicked channels, looking for the best programme and then, joy of joys, there was a Shahrukh Khan New Year special on one channel. After months of misery, Rani felt the load on her heart lift, or perhaps shift, just a little.

Shahrukh Khan smiled, his deep brown eyes the same as ever, he joked, he made self-deprecating remarks and Rani realized she had forgotten how much she loved him. Then he began a performance, dancing to old Kishore Kumar songs. Bittu began to applaud. Rani forgot every worry, every bill and all fatigue. Shahrukh clowned and danced and leapt around the stage with the other performers for over half an hour. Then panting, perspiring and still smiling, he told his audience that he loved them.

Rani believed him.

Then he danced to songs from his own films with various leading ladies. When Kajol appeared on the stage, the lights dimmed, Shahrukh calmed down a little and the two slowly danced to '*Tujhe dekha to yeh jaana sanam*'. Rani suddenly felt that the world was a happy place. She felt teary at the same time. She got to her feet, ran to her father and woke him up, begging him to eat a little and to sit with them for a while. But Dheeraj, his hands trembling, gulped down two glasses of water with more pills and went back to sleep again. This saddened Rani but did not dampen her spirits. When she turned back to the television, Shahrukh was being menacingly cool, dancing as a villain from his film *Don*. Yet he had a smile on his face as if he secretly knew he was being silly. Then a few romantic numbers; he stretched his arms as if he wanted to embrace the whole world. Rani's appetite was back in full form and she and Bittu wolfed down everything. The samosas were lovely and the chowmein tasted great.

Rani decided that she would determine the course of life now. She could not just sit back helplessly and watch things fall apart. After all, what was wrong? Her father was just ill. She would take him to the doctor, get him treated and he'd be perfectly fine, sitting in the verandah in his crisp white kurta-pyjama, reading *Dainik Bhaskar* again. She would speak to Mahesh and Neelam whether they liked it or not and ask them to treat Papaji with more respect. They were not bad; maybe the family had just been under strain. They'd be fine.

During a commercial break, Shahrukh Khan asked everyone to buy Nokia mobile phones and Akshay Kumar, hanging from some place in the sky, swigged Thums Up.

As the last item, Shahrukh Khan energetically danced to a medley of his greatest hits. Rani and Bittu, even though their stomachs were crammed with food, got up and danced with him. They managed to stay up till 1 am, when they dozed off right there, the debris of their feast scattered around and the beautiful people on television still requesting the world to buy things throughout the night.

✧ ✧ ✧

There was a Dr Bhatia in their locality, who worked in a hospital for the first half of the day and then sat in his clinic from 2.30-6.30 pm. Rani explained matters to Asha the next day and Asha agreed to let her go at lunchtime. Rani reached home at two and, as was usual now, found her father in bed. She woke him up, deaf to his protests, and wiped his face, head and hands with a wet towel, something that she often did to Bittu. He tried to fend her off but in vain. She checked for money in her purse, filled a bottle of water from Dheeraj's earthen pot, helped him into his chappals and marched him off to the doctor's.

The waiting room was already overflowing with people, though the doctor had yet to arrive. All the seats in the waiting area had been taken up. Rani went to the general store next door, explained things to them and managed to borrow a small stool. She squeezed it into a tiny corner of the waiting room and Dheeraj sat down on it, the other standing patients looking resentfully at him.

The compounder-cum-assistant-cum-cashier, a hectoring young man, smug in his power, was handing out round metal tokens for patients to go in turn-wise. He looked at his shiny watch and said, 'The doctor will be here any moment.' Rani turned the token in her hand, reading the number on it, and realized that they would have to wait a long time for their turn. The room was chilly and sunless. Everyone waited with their fevers, coughs, pains, cuts and other sudden and accumulated hurts. It was 3.15 and Dr Bhatia had still not made an appearance.

'We should go home,' Dheeraj said. 'This is tiring.'

Rani squeezed his hand. 'Please Papaji, just some more time.'

The clinic was depressing. Dheeraj sipped some water out of his bottle and tried to be patient.

At 3.45 pm Dr Bhatia sailed in like a royal personage, making no eye contact with anyone. The compounder pasted an ingratiating smile on his face and divested the doctor of his bag and coat. The doctor went into his cabin and the compounder began to call people in one by one. Every consultation lasted only about five minutes, but the time still dragged. The air smelt of medication and floor cleaner.

The gloomy afternoon crawled.

At five, a cup of tea was brought in for the doctor in a china cup and a saucer, along with two biscuits. The cabin was silent for fifteen minutes and then the patients started to be called again. Rani went out and bought a cup of tea from a tea stall, holding in frustrated tears, and brought it back to Dheeraj.

He sipped it quietly, his eyes glazed, now apparently switched off from his surroundings.

At six, the doctor got out of his cabin and the compounder helped him into his coat. The remaining patients looked fearful.

'Doctorsaab has to go to the hospital now. Come tomorrow, the rest of you,' the compounder said, as if Doctorsaab didn't have a tongue in his head, Rani thought bitterly. There were murmurs of protest and complaints that went unheeded.

Rani got to her feet in fury. 'You,' she said, pointing her finger at the doctor, shocking everyone in the room. 'You listen to me. My father is unwell. He needs help, understand? He has been waiting here since two.'

The doctor looked at her disdainfully but did not speak. The compounder indignantly caught hold of Rani's elbow, trying to steer her away from the doctor. 'Behave yourself, girl. Everyone who comes here is ill. Do you think Doctorsaab doesn't know that? You people are all the same. He spends all his time curing you and you have no respect for him.'

'He doesn't do it for free,' Rani shouted. 'We pay him. And we all know he rushes off from here to Sharma Private Hospital where he makes his real money.'

The doctor, ignoring her regally, checked his coat for his car keys and left with a curt nod at the compounder, who still gripped Rani's elbow tight.

'Let go of my daughter,' Dheeraj said to the compounder in a dangerously quiet voice. 'Right now.'

Afraid of the quiet voice, the compounder let go of Rani's elbow. Rani could have wept with frustration. With all the courage and dignity she could muster, she gathered her purse and the water bottle, slapped the token down on the reception table, held her father's hand and walked back home, feeling as old and tired as him.

Seventeen

After this sole effort, Dheeraj seemed to have given up and refused to see a doctor. Rani tried to persuade him many times but he would just shake his head. He spent most of his days lying in bed in a stupor. The January days were extremely foggy now and the damp fingers of the fog crept into the house. Dheeraj developed a nasty cough. One Sunday morning, Neelam asked Rani to come and sit by her.

'There is something I need to talk to you about.' Even though Rani found it difficult, she went and sat by Neelam.

'It is about your father,' Neelam began. Rani's mouth tightened. She wasn't going to sit here listening to Neelam criticize Dheeraj.

'I know he is unwell,' she said, rising to her feet, 'and I am trying to take care of him.'

'Sit down,' Neelam said. 'And don't talk as if he has no kith and kin except you.'

Words trembled on Rani's lips. About how some days she was the only person to speak to Dheeraj. How she came home to often find his earthen pot of water empty. How she had noticed that when Dheeraj was asleep, nobody bothered to wake him up to offer him food. She said none of this but Neelam seemed to sense it.

'You think it is all our fault, right? You think I am like those daughters-in-law in television serials who criminally neglect their in-laws. But just see what has happened. The money that we needed to pay for the water tank, the repairs and the painting came out to be 18,500 rupees. I eventually had to borrow it from my brothers. Do you know how ashamed it made me feel? And your brother has begun to look ill, doing overtime at that wretched mill.'

Rani finally spoke, though she tried to keep her emotions in check. 'What is the point of talking about it? It is done now. Look what it has done to Papaji. He is a wreck.'

'But that is what I want to talk to you about,' Neelam said.

'Mahesh and I think he is taking something. Sleeping pills or tranquilizers or something. And he is taking more than he should. That is why he lies in bed all day. It is difficult to talk to him, let alone offer him food and drink.'

Rani was wordless, shocked at the cold way in which Neelam was informing her, as if it was a minor irritant to be taken care of!

There was silence in the room for what seemed like ages.

Then Rani broke the silence. 'But he has a bad cough, too,' she said, defensively, though in an uncertain voice. 'And sometimes his chest and arm hurt and he perspires. He is ill, I know.'

'Maybe he is,' Neelam said patiently. 'But there is not much chance of taking care of any other ailments till he becomes clear-headed, is there?'

Neelam rose. 'Can you imagine what the neighbours and relatives must be thinking? It is shocking, the state he has fallen to. I just thought it my duty to tell you.'

And Neelam went in, with the air of having washed her hands of the whole matter.

It was true, Rani thought. Dheeraj spent all his time in bed floating in and out of sleep. She went in to him. He was awake, silent.

'Papaji,' she said, sitting on the floor beside his bed. 'Bhabhi says you take tranquilizers or sleeping pills or something throughout the day. But nobody prescribed them to you. Then why? You are already ill. They'll weaken you.' Rani tried to keep her voice steady.

Her father lifted a harried face to her. There were dark circles under his eyes and his face was gaunt. 'I don't know how this happened,' he whispered. 'Everything just slipped away. You won't understand.'

'Stop saying I won't understand,' she snapped at him, the pain on his face squeezing her heart. 'I will understand if you tell me.'

'You see,' he said, 'I am not the type.'

'What type?'

'The type to live at all. Especially like this. When the spirit is always in chains. Your mother understood that about me. It made her unhappy too. She would fight with me. But because she understood, I could at least be myself. No one else ever has.'

'But what has this got to do with you making yourself ill? I might not understand everything, Papaji, but I do love you,' Rani said, holding his hand, still trying hard not to cry.

'I didn't know Aman wouldn't return the money. I trusted him. Like I would my own son,' Dheeraj said. 'And these things keep happening. It is not just the money. I am never able to understand what people are thinking, why they say one thing and do another; it is tiring for me to interpret them. I am not fit to live in this world. No wonder Neelam and Mahesh despise me. And rightly so. I have been no good, ever, to anyone.'

'They don't despise you,' Rani said.

'They do,' he answered with a sad smile. 'It is difficult for me to say this because I remember Mahesh when he was a baby, I remember how he cried when he was teething and how he would tilt his head and give us toothless smiles. But they do.'

Rani listened quietly. Only if her father would go on speaking to her, go on and on till every hurt, all confusion had been worded out of his system. But he grew quiet again.

After a minute or so, he spoke again, 'And then … then someone said,' he averted his eyes from her, 'someone said I should take these medicines. They help you sleep.' He looked up at her. 'I am not weak. I am not. Do you think I am?' There was a faint tremor in his jaw. 'No, I don't think so,' Rani said, smoothing his brow, determined that she would help him out of this somehow.

✧ ✧ ✧

Rani was scrubbing a woman's face with apricot scrub before a facial when Dolly came up to her. 'Phone call,' she said softly, and slipped away.

Rani clicked her tongue in exasperation. Bittu was going too far now. He'd get her fired from her job if he didn't stop. Little rascal! Rani couldn't just rush off to attend the call. She waited till she had sponged the woman's face dry and slathered on some cream before excusing herself.

'Hello,' she said fiercely into the phone.

'Rani?'An unfamiliar voice answered. 'It is your uncle.'

Rani recognized his slightly raspy voice now. He was a distant relative. Why was he calling here? How did he know the number?

'Rani, you have to come home. Right now.'

Rani stayed silent.

'It is your father.'

There was a pause. Somebody switched on a hairdryer and the buzz filled Rani's ears.

'Hello. Can you hear me?' Uncle bellowed. 'Your father is dead. Come home. Can you hear me?'

Rani nodded.

'Can you hear me?' he shouted into the phone again.

Rani could hear tempos honking and the ringing of bicycle bells from his side of the line. He must be calling from the PCO near their house.

Rani nodded again.

Bad connection,' she heard him say at the other end of the line. 'I don't think she heard a word. I am not paying for this call.'

Rani hung on to the receiver mutely.

'But the meter is running,' she heard another voice say.

Behind Rani, Kavita dropped a box of hair curlers. 'Uff, now I'll have to sort them into small, medium and large again,' she grumbled.

'You people are all cheats,' Uncle was saying. 'Why should I pay if the call didn't go through?'

'You asked someone to call the girl. I heard you.'

'Bad connection and still two rupees,' Uncle grumbled.

'Go to some other PCO then. But you'll have to pay for this call.'

There was a click as Uncle hung up.

Rani realized her hands were clammy, and so was the receiver she was holding. She hung up then carefully wiped her clammy hands with her chunni, even the spaces between her fingers. She went up to Asha. Asha was doing accounts with her calculator and a notebook in front of her, murmuring to herself. She looked up at Rani and sighed. 'Look, I don't want any more arguments about who damaged the hairdryer,' she said brusquely. 'Go and work. It is a busy day today. Mrs Mehta will be here in fifteen minutes. She just called. Not that she is punctual, but still, get the Shahnaz Hussain facial ready.'

Rani continued to look at her, trying to speak.

'Rani, you are a good girl, but I seriously don't know where your brain lives half the time. Go!'

'No,' Rani said.

Asha looked amazed. Rani had never been impudent before. 'No? What do you mean no?'

'I have to go home,' Rani said. 'Now.'

Asha sighed again. These girls were so touchy you'd think they were princesses. 'See,' she said patiently. 'These things keep happening. I know Dolly said you ruined the hairdryer, but she didn't mean any harm. Don't take it to heart. Okay? Get back to work now, that's a good girl.'

'I have to go home. To my father.'

'To your father?' Asha looked at Rani closely. 'Are you unwell?'

'My father has gone.'

'Where?'

Rani looked blank. Asha finally noticed her pallor and her slightly shaking hands. It scared her. What was the girl talking about?

'Where has he gone, Rani?'

'I don't know,' Rani said, almost in a whisper. 'I don't know where they go.'

Asha stood up. 'What ...?'

✧ ✧ ✧

Rani slowly took off her red-and-white checked apron. She took her purse out of the cupboard, calmly adjusted her chunni in front of the mirror and walked out of the parlour, blank-faced and dry-eyed.

She took an auto without haggling over the price. She felt dizzy. Salman Khan and Katrina Kaif smiled from two stickers on either side of the windshield. A picture of Lord Krishna hung between them. She passed the familiar sights unseeingly – the Shiv temple, the rows of fruit stalls, the hoardings. Rani blinked, trying to look around, trying to make sense.

On a glossy new hoarding for a Samsung phone, Aamir Khan smiled down, saying, 'Next is what?'

✧ ✧ ✧

Even before Rani turned into her street, she could hear the noise. Wails and howls reached her ears. She turned the corner, and her eyes fell on her beloved home. There were people milling around. The small gate, the yard, the front door – all jammed with people. Three women she did not know were squatting outside the house, their heads covered with white chunnis, beating their chests and wailing. Rani moved closer. Each step was an effort. At every step, she could feel one foot make contact with the earth, the other leaving it, one after the other, moving forward. She had never felt so aware of being alive. Her legs felt icy-cold inside the cotton salwar.

Finally, Rani stood right outside her home. Neelam, Mahesh and Bittu were nowhere in sight. Rani spotted Satish's mother, dabbing at her eyes with a neat, ironed handkerchief that had a rose embroidered in a corner. That rose, thought Rani, looked silly. Plain handkerchiefs with a nice lace border looked much better.

The icy January chill seeped through to her bones. Some people fell silent when they saw her, the women began to wail louder and rushed to her, attempting to hug her. She managed to ward them off and squeezed her way inside her home. And there he lay, covered in a white sheet, his feet tied together. Rani stood and watched carefully. This couldn't be happening. This couldn't be him. She walked towards him. Wailing relatives parted to make way for her. She bent down by the sheet-covered form and gently turned the corner of the sheet down from his face. His face was in perfect repose. Rani ran her fingers through his hair and kissed his forehead. It was icy. She finally saw Neelam in a white sari crying in a corner, surrounded by other weeping women. She looked around at the expectant faces around her and felt blank. Then she went to check her father's bed. He wasn't there. Rani went to sit in front of the television and stayed there for a few hours, staring at the blank screen.

✧ ✧ ✧

The cremation was over. The relatives surrounding the burning pyre had reminded Rani of the joyful, jeering crowds that had watched poor Ravan burn. Dheeraj's bones had been picked from the cooled ashes and Mahesh had made a trip to Hardwar with other male relatives to immerse them. The thirteen-day period of mourning had begun. A large framed photograph of Dheeraj's, taken about ten years ago and blown up for the occasion, sat in a corner of the room, incense burning in front of it. White cotton sheets covered the floor, where people came to sit, shed a few tears and offer condolences. Rani did not talk to anyone though she let people hug her and say comforting words.

Instead, she cleared Dheeraj's table of all the medicines on it. She dusted the shelf that held his indifferent gods and polished each idol carefully. She cleaned the brass incense holder and burnt fresh sticks. She changed his sheets, fluffed out his pillow and changed the pillow cover. She scrubbed the room with water into which she dropped some lavender oil from an old bottle that Asha had once given her.

When she opened his brown attaché case, she felt that she could take no more, that she would die too.

But she didn't.

She washed his kurtas and pyjamas while other people prayed and wept, and dried and ironed them. Then she spent a whole day travelling to the leper hospital in Pingalwara to donate his clothes there. She kept his handkerchiefs for herself. At the bottom of the brown attaché case she found a sepia photograph of a young Dheeraj Kumar, smiling, but even then with something unsettling in his eyes. He had an arm awkwardly around his wife's shoulders;

she had a half-smile, the kind you gave to photographers at photo studios. There was the boy Mahesh, standing, holding his mother's hand, looking amazingly like Bittu. Between Dheeraj's knees, Rani saw herself, her eyes saucer-like, a bindi on her forehead for the special occasion. Rani kept the photograph in her own trunk. Every morning, Rani would wash and fill Dheeraj's earthen pot. It was always full now, but she would still empty it and wash it and refill it with fresh water every morning and night.

Some relatives looked askance at Rani's constant activity. But she felt she had to keep moving. People who had thought Dheeraj strange in his lifetime, had taunted him and gossiped about him, now genuflected in front of his portrait and prayed for his soul. Ceremonies took place, from which Rani stayed away. She still hadn't cried.

✧ ✧ ✧

On the fourth day of mourning, Asha arrived with Kavita and Dolly. None of them had been to her place before and had had some trouble locating it.

When they saw Rani she was wearing a pink salwar-kameez that a female relative had rebuked her for. 'Pink is an auspicious colour. If you can't wear white at least wear blue or green or something. At least show that much respect to your father's memory,' she had said. The last time this relative had visited them was when Bittu had been born. Rani had just looked through her.

✧ ✧ ✧

Asha and the girls did not comment on her clothes. Kavita was already crying before she entered the gate, valiantly trying to appear composed. Dolly was blank. Asha, a widow herself, looked calm. She held Rani close to her. Rani's throat felt even tighter than before. She found it difficult to speak.

Kavita said nothing but just sat holding Rani's hand, the silly peacock-shaped ring she was wearing digging into Rani's flesh. Dolly continued to remain blank. They did not talk much but Asha did say softly, 'Have courage. And some faith. The pain will never go away but your heart will become bigger to make place for that pain.' Rani could not reply but she squeezed Asha's hand gratefully. Then Asha said, with her usual brisk change in tone, 'You needn't come to the parlour till the mourning is over. Or take even longer if you need the time. Full pay, of course. And don't feel you are alone, okay? Call us if you need something. The other girls send their love. They will come tomorrow; somebody had to remain at the parlour.' Rani could just nod. Eve's Beauty Parlour seemed a lifetime away to Rani. She pictured Navpreet in charge, trying to get Shama and Mani to be efficient and sensible. She pictured the women who would still be sitting there, getting their eyebrows shaped and agonizing over their hair. It occurred to Rani that Asha must have abandoned or rescheduled at least one bride for this visit.

Rani looked around at the few scattered relatives and the white cotton sheets and said, 'No, I'd like to come to work tomorrow.'

'You can't,' Asha said. 'You won't be able to.'

'Please let me,' Rani said, meeting Asha's eyes with a steady gaze. Asha bit her nails for a moment, thinking, and then nodded at Rani.

'Okay, if that is what you feel like. But you can go home any time you please.'

The three left soon after.

Rani heard Kavita's voice floating back from the gate, reproaching Dolly.

'You could have at least hugged her. Sitting there like a lizard on the wall.'

Then the three women disappeared from sight.

Neelam was angry that Rani wanted to go back to work. She tried to persuade her to wait for a few days. But her words washed over Rani. To her, the world had become like a television set with the sound muted. When she had to listen to something, she had to make an effort to turn the volume up.

Seema next door had been a great friend. She had spoken very little to Rani, had kept Bittu at her place for long hours, even feeding and bathing him, trying to get his mind off his real life. Bittu had not asked anybody any questions and seemed to be pretending that nothing had happened.

The next morning Rani went to work. The potholes, the auto tempos, the stalls had all remained the same. Only she had changed. The girls greeted her warmly with hugs. But Asha had instructed them not to mention her loss unless she brought it up herself.

The first customer Rani had to attend to said to her, 'I need my upper lip and eyebrows threaded. But I was thinking, I don't want a round arc in my eyebrows. I think I would prefer a V-shaped arc, if you know what I mean.'

Rani felt an insane desire to laugh. But she said, 'Yes, that would suit your natural eyebrow shape better.'

The woman sat down with a smile. Rani dabbed talcum powder on the thin strip of skin between her nose and mouth with a piece of cotton wool. Then she expertly twisted the nylon thread around her finger and trained her eyes carefully on the small area of flesh. Rani looked down at the intent way the woman tautened the skin with her tongue. And she felt an affection and a fury at the trivialness of humans. Ten minutes later, the upper lip and the eyebrows were both done. Rani straightened up.

'Perfect,' the woman said, pleased, examining her face in the mirror.

Rani smiled.

✧ ✧ ✧

On the final day of mourning the mats were rolled up, the meagre furniture restored to the room, and the regular household routine resumed.

When Rani went to dust and clean Dheeraj's room, she found his big framed photograph hung on the wall above his own bed. He smiled quietly at his tiny universe of the single bed, the little gods and the few yellowing books. At this sight Rani sank to the floor and, laying her head on his bed, she hugged his pillow and wept and wept, finally acknowledging that she would not ever hear her father's voice again. Or feel the warmth of his hand. Or hear him clear his throat.

She finally realized that Dheeraj Kumar, who had also been her father, was not anymore one of the billions of people walking on the face of the earth. He had gone.

Eighteen

Rani sat with Bittu in front of the TV, watching *Baazigar* listlessly on Zee Cinema. It was late in the evening but Mahesh wasn't back yet. Neelam was in the bedroom folding Mahesh's clothes.

A few months had passed since Dheeraj had died. The cold winter had disappeared, spring had passed by unnoticed and now the days were hot and dry.

On the surface, everything seemed normal. The household routine had resumed as before. But one part of Rani's mind, while she worked in the parlour, watched television or helped in the kitchen, was constantly in an altered state.

A slow, consuming rage had become her constant companion. Memories of slights and injuries to her father, that she had been big enough to ignore while he had been alive, now haunted her every waking moment, not even letting her grieve in peace.

She had begun to resent both Neelam and Mahesh. And she had finally begun to admit it to herself. After Dheeraj's death Mahesh had been morose but Neelam had gone on as if nothing had happened. Rani lay awake during long nights of torment, going over various incidents in the past.

✧ ✧ ✧

One evening, when she returned from the parlour, the door was open. She entered the main room and put down her purse and water bottle. She went to the corner sink to wash her hands and face. And then she heard the two talking. The door of Mahesh and Neelam's room was slightly ajar and she could hear every word they said clearly.

'She will be twenty-two soon,' Mahesh said. 'We should start looking now. It is difficult to get suitable boys these days. And she is such a difficult person at times.'

'All that is fine,' Neelam said acidly. 'But who is going to pay for her wedding? My brothers?'

Mahesh said angrily, 'Of course not. But we still have to get this done. If we don't, people will talk. They'll say that she has no parents and that we are not bothered about her. I just don't want to hear that kind of talk. Not after I have slaved for this family. Really, I expected better from my father.'

Rani's resentment turned to a clear sense of final betrayal at these words. It was as if all this time she had been living with strangers. Strangers who were talking about her impersonally. As if she were no more than an inconvenient problem to be solved.

She stood at the sink rubbing her soapy hands over each other, still listening.

Neelam spoke next. 'Papaji was bad enough, and she seems to have inherited something of his spirit. Trust me, if we don't marry her off quickly, she will just give us trouble.'

'That is what I am saying', Mahesh said wearily. 'But we have to find a good match first.'

'My sister-in-law's cousin is of marriageable age. Just has a slight drinking problem. But they have their own shop,' Neelam said.

Mahesh said uncertainly, 'I don't know if he'd be suitable for her.'

Neelam said indignantly, 'Why not? It isn't as if she is particularly beautiful, though she is not ugly. And, after all, she is just ninth-pass and works at a beauty parlour. In that household, she'll be able to queen it over everyone. What better can we get for her? Especially after Papaji made sure that he left behind no money or good reputation.'

'Besides,' she added, 'she is too strong-willed for a girl. Too many opinions. I am not sure if she is a good influence on our Bittu.'

The words fell like silent blows on Rani's ears. The pink Lux soap lather on her hands was dry now but she continued to rub them together in soaping motions numbly. She couldn't believe her ears. This was her brother with whom she had made mud cakes in the same courtyard outside. The bhabhi she used to hug every morning. And Bittu, her precious little Bittu. She remembered when he had been born. Rani had taken it upon herself to take utmost care of the mother and baby. She had bathed him, dressed him, rocked him to sleep in her arms and, as he grew up, she had covered his notebooks with the mandatory brown paper at the start of every academic year. Every Sunday she had massaged his head with coconut oil, she had taught him multiplication tables, played and laughed with him. They had eaten together, slept together and watched television together. He was her friend, her companion, her baby. And she was supposed to be a bad influence on him? What had she done?

And how could they discuss her marriage in that tone? Wasn't she loved, then? She felt desolate. She looked around the familiar room where she had grown up, at hers and Bittu's mattresses, drawn and scribbled over, at the battered television set, at all the familiarity of home. And in one moment, she felt completely alien. It was as if she had been living an illusion till now. It had disappeared suddenly, leaving her with nothing. Even the name 'Rani' seemed unfamiliar, as if belonging to a happy, carefree girl she vaguely knew or met everyday when out vegetable shopping.

Neelam's voice rose again. 'I don't want to be disrespectful but Papaji really disgraced us. If we at least get her married off, maybe we will have some peace and will be able to hold up our heads in the neighbourhood again.'

Without bothering to wash the dried-up soap on her hands, Rani barged into their room.

With all the dignity that she could muster, she said, 'You needn't bother about my future. I will be leaving.'

The two stared at her, amazed. 'What do you mean? Leaving for where?' Mahesh asked.

'I will decide,' Rani said, almost regally, though she felt like sobbing. 'But I'll leave.'

She threw a withering look at Neelam, 'So that I am not a bad influence on your son,' and then another look at Mahesh, 'and so that your sister does not disgrace you and your wife like your father did.'

Not trusting herself to speak further, Rani left the house and walked around the neighbourhood for two hours. Then, exhausted, she went to Seema and in a few words told her everything. Seema did not try to make her change her mind or give her any advice. She sat in silence for many minutes with her friend and then said tentatively, 'I know you won't be able to tolerate living here any longer. I have an idea, but it is just an idea.'

'What?' Rani asked desperately.

'I have a second cousin, Vina. She lost her parents when she was a child. They lived in Delhi. A kind woman took her in as a domestic help and now she does the same work at a better house. The lady she works for has fractured her leg and they need another maid fast. She wanted me to go, but these people at home kicked up a fuss and wouldn't let me. Said it wasn't respectable. But maybe you could go?'

Rani's face paled, 'You mean, as a servant?'

Seema nodded. 'But that is not my idea,' Seema said, growing excited. 'For one thing, servants there live like queens – own room, eating whatever the family eats, fixed tasks and all. Besides, my idea is, you go to Delhi and work there in that house till you find a good job in a good parlour there. No?' Her eyes were shining now.

Rani looked uncertain. It sounded like such a big move. She had never been out of Amritsar before. But then everything else had changed too. So why not the city.

'Let me think about it.' Rani said. 'But one way or the other, I will get out of this house. I want a house of my own.'

Seema smiled, 'For that, you will have to marry.'

Rani's eyes looked steely. 'Not necessarily.'

✧ ✧ ✧

The next day at the parlour, Rani sought Asha's advice. She told her all and Asha considered things carefully before answering. 'I can understand your feelings. But please remember that it is not easy for a girl to make her way alone in life on her own. What you can do …' said Asha, brightening, 'is that you can continue to work here and I can rent you the room above the garage. That way it will remain respectable too.' Rani thought it over. And in a flash she knew what would happen if she did this. She said to Asha, 'You have just made things clear to me. If I do as you say and take up your very kind offer, my family and numerous relatives in Amritsar will just think that I am sulking. Somebody will come to fetch me before every family function. Family elders will visit and plague and persuade me to do as they say. Also, they'll be unpleasant to you, blaming you for leading me astray. I'll go to Delhi. I'll work hard. Papaji always said that no work was lowly as long as you did it honestly and well. And hopefully I will find a job in a beauty parlour soon.'

The two fell silent for a moment, knowing that this meant that parting was near. By the next day, Asha had told all the other girls too. They suddenly became more formal with her, even a little wary with the exception of Kavita who wailed, 'You'll miss my wedding. Oh, she'll miss my wedding,' turning to Asha for support.

'Be quiet, Kavita,' Asha said quietly. 'These are hard times for her. You can always send her your wedding pictures.'

Kavita seemed consoled by this.

✧ ✧ ✧

Once her mind was made up, Rani lost no time in making the remaining arrangements. Seema spoke to her cousin, Vina. Vina spoke to her employer. The employer, a woman who thought that the Delhi maids were too fast, welcomed the idea. Rani was given an address and was instructed to reach New Delhi on 2 April and take an auto to the address, the fare of which would be reimbursed by the employer. Rani took leave of everyone at Eve's Beauty Parlour, booked her railway ticket and packed up her few belongings. And then came the most difficult part.

The thought of parting with Bittu, leaving her childhood home and all the memories of her father behind tore Rani's heart apart.

She was debating how to break the news to Bittu when he came one evening, angrily rushing at her like a mad bull. He butted her stomach with his head and burst into tears. 'Ma says you are going away,' he wailed loud enough for the whole mohalla to hear. 'Seema Bua also said so. I shan't let you. You want me to rot in school while you roam around. I will come with you. Who will tell me stories?' Rani tried to calm him down at which Bittu dropped all pretence of anger and indignation and started sobbing heartbreakingly like the little boy he actually was. He fell into Rani's lap and cried till he had exhausted himself. He reminded Rani of when he had been three years old. Rani cradled him in her arms like a baby, kissing him all over his grimy face, tears pouring out of her own eyes. She managed to get some hot milk into him and he went to sleep curled up in her lap. Rani could feel his heart thud under her palm and smell the mix of sweat and oil from his scalp. She closed her eyes and fell into a tired slumber. Not even Neelam, who discovered them half an hour later, dared to wake them up.

Mahesh and Neelam had tried very hard to dissuade Rani from leaving, mainly because they didn't want to lose face in the community. They had been coaxing, stern, sentimental in turns. But now Rani was grim, hard and unhearing.

On the morning of 2 April, Rani got up at dawn. Her train was at 6 am. She left a sleeping Bittu after praying to Lord Ganesh, Shiv, Hanuman and Krishna to always protect him. She moved him a little and tugged the bedcover aside. She took a long look at the drawings on his mattress. Apart from monkeys and bicycles there were now headmasters and ceiling fans, cows and bridges, and a smiling fish that wore a crown on its head and a polka-dotted sari.

Rani took one bag full of her belongings and Dheeraj Kumar's brown attaché case with its books, photographs and other assorted possessions.

And, leaving the household asleep, she took a rickshaw alone to the Amritsar railway station.

Nineteen

Rani's eyes were dry. The train was late and she had been waiting for hours. The hot wind that blew over the sweat-stained people on the crowded platform stung them. She rubbed them. The platform was crawling with people. Waves of people and sounds unnerved her and she felt dizzy again. It was just the beginning of April, but already the heat was unbearable. Fans hung by long holders at regular intervals on the platform but the space under each of them was taken up by sprawled families, the children's faces covered with their mother's chunnis to keep the buzzing flies off. A clean, air-conditioned first-class waiting room was visible. Through thick glass, Rani could see well-dressed men with briefcases sitting on chairs, tapping their feet impatiently. A lone woman in a pant suit, the kind Rani had seen women wearing in magazines, sat in a corner, punching a number furiously into a cellphone. Rani found an empty, shaded place close to a food stall and sat down. She realized that her hands were trembling slightly.

She looked around and noticed several children, some asleep, shaded by their mothers' pallus, others running around aimlessly, excited by every new thing they encountered, still others playing in exhilaration in the freedom they were unused to till their exasperated, harassed mothers slapped or coaxed them back into their folds.

Rani felt a sharp pang with a sudden remembrance of the feel of Bittu sleeping next to her, his bony knees often dirty, mouth slightly open and with an arm carelessly flung over her. Then she clenched her trembling hands. She fiercely told herself that she would no longer think of things that hurt, of beloved people gone from this world, or separated from her in what seemed like a randomly cruel move on life's part. She would no longer think of abandoned idols on shelves or paper boats. Nothing.

The train she had to take to Delhi had still not arrived on the platform. Her mind churned. The chaos within her and the one in the outside world, together, were too much for her. Rani longed for the train to come, almost as if by boarding it, she could leave her storm of emotions on the platform behind, along with the squalling children, hysterical passengers and aggressive vendors. Her eyes fell on a copy of *Filmfare* outside the magazine stand. It had Ranbir Kapoor on the cover. Rani mechanically remembered that she had always been a little suspicious and resentful of him, suspecting him of planning to take over Shahrukh Khan's number-one position.

Next to the magazine stand, a derelict-looking woman lay asleep. As Rani watched, she stirred, put a grimy hand into a bag and took out a Coke bottle filled with water. After a few swigs she went back to sleep. The glare of the sun was getting worse. The memories of her father, Bittu, Shahrukh Khan and the woman before her – nothing added up. Nothing made sense anymore. Rani hid her face in her hands and stared into the dark of her palms till her train finally arrived.

✧ ✧ ✧

'Do you want an aloo parantha? One?' the woman sitting across Rani urgently asked her husband. The train had not yet begun to move.

He did not answer. He was squatting, trying to fit his luggage under the seat. The woman held a multi-storied steel tiffin box affectionately in her lap.

'Forget the paranthas,' he said tersely. 'Just control that child.'

The boy, who seemed about three years old, stood by the window experimentally licking at the iron bars. Rani had the other window seat.

Three more men joined their compartment, daily commuters who got off at Jalandhar. They wordlessly whipped out a pack of cards and began playing, affectionately swearing at each other intermittently. And finally, the train began to move out of the station. Rani turned her head to the window and finally let silent tears leak out as Amritsar began to fade away from her eyes.

Two hours later the businessmen had got off at Jalandhar, to be replaced by a thin Sikh man who prayed for the entire journey, his eyes shut, hands folded in his lap, his lips moving wordlessly. The couple had contentedly finished the aloo paranthas; the woman offered Rani one with a friendly smile, but Rani declined. The child slept through most of the journey and, by evening, the train had reached the outskirts of Delhi. It remained stationary there for an hour. This made the man impatient and irritated with his wife and he snapped at everything she said. Rani tried to pretend that she could not see or hear them. She looked out of the window – slums of the sort she had never seen before lined the railway tracks. Goats and children ran among cooking pots. Rani thought that perhaps she ought to be grateful that she was just poor, not bitterly poor. A man sitting on his haunches, smoking a beedi, gazed into the cloudless sky. In the compartment the man snapped yet once more. The wife muttered, 'My father never spoke to my mother like that.' And for the remaining time that the train stood there, she sniffed and sulked.

It was a good half hour before the train stirred again.

II

One

Sadhna woke up to the thud of the rolled-up newspaper hitting against the glass window behind her, to a darkish-dawnish light.

This was how she had been waking up every day for the last twenty days. She could hear the traffic; her bed might as well as have been parked on the main road. She kept meaning to meet this boy or man some day and ask him to aim at anywhere except the window, but had never managed to. Sadhna opened her eyes, not wanting to face another morning, a morning that couldn't be heard above the roar of the traffic.

The new girl, Rani, she thought, would be arriving today. Sadhna fervently hoped that she would be less talkative and less tiring than Vina, the young girl who cooked and cleaned for her.

The trouble had begun in the very first week that Sadhna had moved into the house. One afternoon, Vina was brushing the carpet in the living room where Sadhna sat on the couch reading Saul Bellow's *Herzog*. Her hair was tied up anyhow with one of those silly elastic things called scrunchies. She was wearing her reading glasses and a lavender nightdress, a gift from a former boyfriend that now looked ridiculous with her leg in a plaster.

The copy of *Herzog* she was reading was an old one picked up from a second hand book market. The print was small and Sadhna had to strain to read.

> Late in spring, Herzog had been overcome by the need to explain, to have it out, to justify, to put in perspective, to clarify, to make amends.

'Memsaab?' Vina said.

Sadhna groaned. 'Don't call me "memsaab". Address me by my name.' Vina looked shocked and said, 'I can't do that!' in a horrified tone.

'Well then, at least call me something else.'

'Didi?' Vina asked. 'Can I call you Didi?'

'Whatever. Just don't call me "*memsaab*".'

Sadhna went back to her book, trying to concentrate again. She managed to read a page. The carpet brushing went on.

> He went on taking stock, lying face down on the sofa. Was he a clever man or an idiot? Well, he could not at this time, claim to be clever.

'Didi?' Vina interrupted chirpily. 'Where are you from? I mean, originally.'

Sadhna sighed. 'Dhanbad. I was born there. It is in a state called Jharkhand.'

'Isn't Patna close by? I have relatives there. An aunt with three sons. One son drinks and beats his wife. The second lives only for two things – films and cricket. Only the last-born is of any comfort to her.' Vina absentmindedly smoothed her hair with the carpet brush. 'Nobody ever knows with boys,' she continued. 'They can turn out any way. Do you have a brother?' she asked conversationally. Sadhna wondered if the girl ever shut up.

'No,' she answered.

Vina looked a little put out, then asked, 'Husband?'

'No.'

'Oh well, life without men is difficult. But life with men is also difficult. That is what my aunt from Patna always says.' Vina went back to the carpet. It was clean now but she wanted to hang around Sadhna a little longer.

Sadhna read on:

> He might once have had the makings of a clever character but he had chosen to be dreamy instead, and the sharpies cleaned him out.

Sadhna was touched by this sentence.

'Didi,' Vina piped up again. 'I have broken my cup. Can you please give me another?'

Sadhna looked mystified.

'Take another,' she said. 'There is a whole set in the kitchen, right?'

'No, no, I mean *my* cup,' Vina said. 'Just for me to drink in.'

Then Sadhna figured out what Vina meant. Most middle-class Hindu households in India kept separate plates and glasses for domestic help, backward castes and Muslims.

'No, no, you needn't do all that,' she said. 'You can eat and drink from any plate or glass. Use anything in the kitchen.'

Vina looked a little shocked but gratified.

'And ... um ...' Sadhna added awkwardly, 'you don't have to sit on the floor all the time. Be comfortable. You live here. Treat it like your own home.'

Vina nodded primly, her face impassive, but her heart full of delight at the prospect of all the forbidden pleasures she could indulge in now, pleasures that no previous employer had ever allowed. With a slight frown of impatience, Sadhna continued to read. She read for about five minutes and then Vina asked, 'Can I watch TV too?'

'Hm,' Sadhna nodded absently, wishing the girl would shut up.

Unknown to her, Vina, though pleased, began to lose respect for Sadhna. What kind of a memsahib was this?

✧ ✧ ✧

It was to this somewhat strange household that Rani came, to take up her new position as a maid. When Rani's auto trundled to a stop in front of the house, she checked the nameplate, and then the paper in her hand, to see if it was the right address. It was. Rani fumbled with her luggage and her money. She absently noticed a postcard of Sachin Tendulkar stuck with multiple strips of sellotape above the windshield of the auto rickshaw. Rani's hands were clammy with nervousness. She paid the auto driver the impossibly high sum of hundred rupees that he had asked for.

The driver, an absent look on his face too, casually pocketed the money and trundled off on his endless, tiring journey again.

Rani took a deep breath and looked up at the imposing house. She couldn't believe she had made such a long journey alone. Despite the bewildering New Delhi Railway Station, despite the chaos and the touts, despite the terrifying auto-rickshaw ride through roads that she did not know, she had made it.

And now that she was here, all her courage abruptly deserted her. She did not want to ring the bell. She wanted to sit down and cry till Papaji, Seema or Shahrukh Khan came and comforted her and took her away to a safe, happy place. A passing colony watchman gave her a suspicious, appraising look.

Mustering up both dignity and courage, Rani pressed the bell, a white switch that had an elaborate red bell drawn on it. A slim, flamboyant girl come out of the door, walked to the imposing white gate and asked cheerily, 'Rani?'

Rani nodded. Vina ushered her in.

Her heart thudding against her ribs, Rani entered the strange house.

✧ ✧ ✧

Vina took Rani in to introduce her to Sadhna. Rani followed her down a driveway lined with potted plants, through a massive, carved wooden door, into a hallway that was dim and then into a medium-sized, sunlit room.

Rani saw a woman in a chair, her hair untidy and clothes worn and old, who had evidently not been to a beauty parlour in ages. She had a plaster on her right leg and a book on her lap. Every surface near her was covered with books and papers. She looked up when Rani entered. Her eyes were deep brown and warm.

'Namaste,' Rani said politely, trying to fold her hands without dropping her luggage.

'Namaste,' Sadhna said. 'How was your journey? Tiring?'

Rani shook her head. Then she ran her tongue over her dry lips. Rani knew what a sight she must make!

She wore her hair in its customary plait. She wore a blue salwar-kameez, the cloth at the armpits wet with sweat. Above each ear, she had tidily pulled back her hair with red plastic ladybird hairclips out of which some strands had escaped now. There was a tremor in her hands that clutched her paltry luggage; Vina relieved her of it.

On her thin wrist was still the solitary silver bangle she had worn for over a year.

Rani nervously fiddled with the old bangle. Strange, she thought, how innocuous objects outlived living, breathing people.

To Sadhna, she appeared unnaturally white-faced and exhausted. 'Vina, give her something to drink. Water and then some fruit juice. And then let her wash and rest,' Sadhna said, smiling warmly at Rani. 'These summer journeys are very tiring. Rest today. Tell me if you need anything – clothes or a toothbrush or comb or anything like that. You can start work tomorrow.'

Rani just nodded back with an attempt at a smile.

Beneath her nervousness, she felt a little defiant. Kindness was fine, but she did not want any charity.

And she had her own toothbrush.

✧ ✧ ✧

Vina introduced herself cheerfully to Rani and showed her the room they were both supposed to share. Then she left her alone to wash and rest.

Rani looked around at the Bittu-less room. It was a simple, clean room, though the paint on the walls was peeling. There were two single wooden beds in it, perpendicular to each other. One had clothes and face cream scattered on it. Rani assumed it was the other girl, Vina's bed. The other bed was by the window, covered with a clean, threadbare sheet and a thin pillow. A Lord Shiv calendar and a poster of Aamir Khan adorned the walls. There was a minuscule attached bathroom-cum-toilet. It contained a bucket and a mug and was cluttered with Vina's cheap cosmetics and toiletries. There was a ventilator high up in the wall where some birds had made a nest. Rani heard a bird chirp, then all was silent again except for the continuous, extraordinarily loud, unfamiliar roar of the traffic. Rani put her things down.

The room was so, so empty.

But she would not cry. She did not have the energy. And the day was too hot. Slightly unnerved, Rani, trying to calm herself, took a cold bucket bath in the small bathroom. After she had scrubbed herself clean, she let mugfuls of water trickle down slowly from the top of her head to the spaces between her toes.

After her bath, Rani stood in the middle of the new room, looking around blankly at the walls, not having a clue as to what she was doing here.

Two

Sadhna did not know when and why the germ of writing had crept into her organism insidiously. She always remembered being at odds with her surroundings, aware of a void, aware of the illusions of the world. Reading was her only succour. Writing had been the next logical step to attempt to create some sense of the chaos around her.

Meanwhile, practical life had to go on. Sadhna's father was a respectable engineer in the PWD and her mother was a schoolteacher. Sadhna finished her schooling in Dhanbad with decent marks, sat for various entrance exams and ended up at an engineering college in Bangalore for a four-year degree in Information Science and Technology.

To Sadhna, it mattered little what course she was doing. She lived in a private women's hostel, and was delighted to find that a city could contain so many bookstores and libraries. For the next four years, she spent difficult hours at college, learning computer programming, drawing circuit diagrams and doing, what seemed to her, pointless experiments in laboratories. While hooking up wires, jotting down readings from voltmeters, waiting for this light to flash on or that circuit to be completed, one part of her mind would be dwelling on a story she was writing or the novel she was reading.

She couldn't wait to get back to her room to read and write. Young men who showed interest in her seemed mere children. She had a relationship with an older architect. She outgrew that, too, always coming back faithfully to her world of words.

It was in her last year of college that the inevitable happened. As the final part of her course, the students had to do a project in an outside company, in twos or threes. The place she had to go to for this was an hour's ride away by bus in the rush hour. So she would arm herself with a book everyday to read on the way to Alpha Electronics and back. One day, she was so engrossed in a volume of Saadat Hasan Manto's short stories that she almost forgot to get down at her stop. She hurriedly got down and stood there, clutching the book in her hand. She had to cross the road to enter Alpha Electronics. She looked up at the building and envisioned what awaited her. Enthusiastic students, rows of computers, JAVA and Oracle, talk of campus placements, Siemens, Wipro, a job in America perhaps, marriage ...

And then she looked down at the book she was holding, one finger inserted in it to mark the page she was on. She withdrew her finger. It was red with the pressure. And Sadhna knew then that even if she did finish this course, there was nothing she could do after it except write. Absolutely nothing.

And so Sadhna rejected a corporate career and marriage and immersed herself in reading and writing with the bloody-mindedness that only the young can have. She did not know what elusive glimmer of truth she was looking for. For four years, she lived in rented rooms in various cities and wrote on rented computers, refusing her worried parents' help in an effort to be independent. She tutored, did odd jobs.

And then, one day, in a damp, small room she had rented, she sat staring at the computer. Her first novel was complete.

What happened next was a fluke. Her manuscript, which she had sent to a few friends for feedback, ended up in the hands of a man with some influence in the Western literary circles. He liked it enough to send it to an agent and before Sadhna knew what was happening, the manuscript got sold, was translated into many languages and was written well about.

Sadhna was hailed by some as the new 'literary find' of India.

Journalists praised her.

She was given several awards.

She made several trips to Delhi for interviews, finally drifting to a rented room in the city.

The book was launched in a big way.

She went to other cities for book readings and promotion.

Her name appeared in newspapers.

All this while, Sadhna felt a vague discomfort that she could not place.

She was jolted out of her paper-and-pen world into the Real World.

Sadhna was plunged into the world of writers, artists, critics and journalists of all kinds. Everyone had an opinion. They were all over the place – in magazines, on talk shows, at each other's book launches and exhibitions. There was no self-doubt or hesitancy. In India, where only a handful of people could speak and write in English, a bunch of people with a facility of the language had appropriated literature, ruthlessly running the business along with their Western counterparts. The bearded and the bindi-ed of Delhi had set themselves up as the intelligentia, satisfied in their incestuous circle, without foraying into unknown territories.

Everyone was on the make, with an eye on the main chance.

It was a joke. A very sad one.

And Sadhna realized that she had lost the ability to write. Her little god of literature had been snatched away. Literature was not, as she had thought, a truthful, pure place where you could work hard to filter away the lies.

It was a lie itself now, living in a savage marketplace.

Sadhna kept writing doggedly, but now that she could hear the strident, confident voices all around her, she felt unable to make her voice heard over them. Not being able to write was like being unable to wipe steam off a bathroom mirror.

An act that should be easy, simple, but she couldn't.

She slid deeper and deeper into a dark pit of gloom where words made no sense to her. The very words that had once liberated her now seemed like adversaries, cunningly designing themselves to lie, conceal and lead astray. Still searching for that elusive glimmer of truth, Sadhna retreated. She became that tortured being – a stalled novelist.

Some wrote her off as a one-book wonder. Some said she had mismanaged her career badly. After such a successful novel she should have belted out another in a couple of years, she should have made contacts, she should have attended book launches and seminars to stay in public memory.

Sadhna had not played her cards well.

Because all she had wanted to do was tell a story – as simply and truthfully as she could.

✧ ✧ ✧

Rani came down the next morning, as nervous, fresh and clean as a new schoolgirl. She didn't know what to do with herself. She missed the familiarity of Eve's Beauty Parlour where you knew what to do as soon as you entered, where to head, where everything was placed and what would get you into trouble. Vina, who was already down, smiled at her. She was scrubbing the marble slabs of the kitchen counter clean. She hoped that this new girl would be fun. It bored her to work alone in the house.

'Memsaab,' Vina began then stopped herself. 'No, she does not like us to call her 'memsaab'. We must call her Didi. So *Didi* has said that this morning we can have our tea with her, in case you are homesick or something.'

Rani nodded again. Vina felt a little exasperated. Did the girl have a tongue in her mouth at all? Vina put a pan of water on the gas and, when it boiled, she deftly threw in tea leaves, milk and sugar. Rani watched numbly.

Within ten minutes, the two girls went to the living room where Sadhna was immersed in a copy of *Alice in Wonderland*. Vina settled herself comfortably on the carpet. Sadhna, noticing the uncertainty on Rani's face, motioned her to follow suit.

'You are from Amritsar, right Rani?' Sadhna asked. Rani nodded.

'And what did you do before coming here?'

Rani stared out of the window thinking of potholes in roads, kites flying high in the sky, head massages and hairdryers and night-time stories. She did not reply but Sadhna saw tears glisten in her eyes. Sadhna had gathered that there had been some difficult circumstance in the girl's life before she came here. So she decided not to probe further.

'Just treat this like your home, okay?' She said. 'Have your tea before it gets cold,' she said, sipping at her own cup.

Vina felt happy, ensconced in the household in the superior position of the insider, and looked at Rani with some pity.

'The tea is a little strange today,' Sadhna said. 'A bit too strong, perhaps?'

'Well,' Vina sighed. 'I asked you not to buy Brooke Bond Red Label.'

Sadhna began to say something sharp but stopped herself.

'No, it isn't that. Just don't let it brew for too long. Okay?'

Vina looked into her cup as if she and her cup of tea understood each other in a way that Sadhna never could. Then Vina turned to Rani. 'Do you like watching television?'

The Shahrukh Khan concert on New Year's Eve … the benign preacher on Aastha channel, who Papaji loved … the claims and fights over the remote control …

'No,' Rani said stiffly.

'You should watch some TV,' Vina said wisely, 'otherwise with just three people in the house, the house will seem dead.'

This time Sadhna did speak a little sharply.

'Don't be absurd, Vina. There are other things to do besides watching television.'

Vina's face fell a little. Sadhna turned to Rani.

'Did you like your room?' she asked her. Rani nodded.

'Let me know if there is anything you need. Vina will tell you your duties.' Then, in an attempt to lighten Rani's mood, Sadhna said, 'I am not usually so lazy. But,' here she pointed to her plaster, 'for a while you two will have to do everything for me.'

'Does it hurt?' Rani asked in a very quiet voice.

'Not much,' Sadhna said. 'But it is a nuisance. And it is not much fun when you can't move about and have to rely on others even to get you water.'

Rani thought of Papaji. 'Yes, it is not.'

Rani then added in a suddenly stronger voice, as if taking charge, 'Don't worry. I will take care of you.'

Sadhna was surprised. Vina did not look too pleased.

✧ ✧ ✧

'How did you get the fracture?' Rani managed to ask Sadhna later that evening. She had spent the day hanging around Vina, who showed her the kitchen, the contents of its various shelves and cabinets, the cupboard under the stairs where all the cleaning materials, mops and dusters were stored. Rani had had trouble keeping up; she was tired and she found Vina exhaustingly lively and animated. She spent the day in a daze and was relieved when Sadhna summoned her and requested her to help shift her to the bedroom.

She had felt moved at the pain in Sadhna's eyes as she clumsily settled herself in bed and could not help asking her.

Sadhna was about to merely laugh and dismiss it as a minor accident when she saw the genuine concern in the girl's deep, serious eyes.

'I dislike the Delhi roads, so they dislike me back. I had an accident. Just the law of the universe,' Sadhna answered. Rani nodded understandingly, and quietly began to tuck the bedclothes around her. Sadhna was pleasantly surprised by the understanding nod, the silence. She thought back to last month. She had been on her way to a meeting with an editor, a good-looking woman called Antara, hoping to sell her a story that she had just finished writing. That was when she had met with the accident.

Antara had come to visit her in the hospital. Good-naturedly, but with a slightly bullying manner, she had told Sadhna that she could no longer stay in her second-floor flat, alone and unattended. She knew of an academic couple who were going to Oxford for three months and wanted to let their spacious, sprawling home to someone. They didn't want much rent, they just wanted their house to be occupied and kept in running order. Since Sadhna, as usual, was low on cash, she thought it wasn't a bad idea.

'A maid goes with the house,' Antara had said briskly. 'You might have to employ another though, since you will be completely immobile.' The idea of having maids was unnerving since Sadhna had mostly lived alone and was used to doing her own chores, but she didn't have much of a choice.

Sadhna had agreed. She had at first found the large, expensively furnished house in a posh colony quite daunting. And Vina tired her. For the first time in this house, as she felt Rani's cold fingers brush against her foot while tucking her in, Sadhna felt a degree of comfort. She liked Rani.

✧ ✧ ✧

And so, Rani began her days as a household help. It was strange for her to live in a new house, get used to unfamiliar objects and smells, strange to share a room with Vina instead of with Bittu. After the bustling atmosphere of Eve's Beauty Parlour and Bittu as a companion at home, Sadhna and the house seemed as dead and listless to Rani as did her own self. When she was sent to buy vegetables in the mornings, she missed the familiar marketplaces of Amritsar. Instead, all she saw were large houses with drivers washing cars. Each household seemed to have three cars. And there would be servants from the colony walking pedigreed dogs on leashes. The dogs wore expensive sweaters and the people walking them looked malnourished. It was all very alien to her.

For the next few weeks, Rani alternated between grief, numbness and anger. They went on and on, inexorably, cyclically, one following the other. There was no respite for her. The housework helped sometimes. It relieved her closed-up spirit to scrub away at floors and dishes with all her strength. On other days, when she would be sponging non-stick pans with liquid Vim cleaner or chopping onions while her eyes watered, she would feel bitter. Here she was, no matter how anyone worded it, a mere *servant*, someone who could have been a teacher if she had listened to her father. Even her beauty-parlour skills lay wasted.

When Rani lay down to sleep in her bed each night, it was always the worst moment of her day. She would miss home, she would miss Bittu, the story-telling, the forbidden drawings on the mattress, his non-stop talk that made her beg him to stop so she could sleep. And she missed the comforting small body next to her.

✧ ✧ ✧

The morning tea was a bit of ritual. For the first few days, Rani was just busy learning the ropes, getting used to the pace and the rhythm of her new life. Vina usually took care of the tea making. Then one morning she said to Rani, 'I'll brew a cup of tea for memsaab, and you bring in two Britannia Marie biscuits and a piece of toast on a tray. That way, you'll get used to everything.'

Rani nodded, but then said, 'I don't know how to use a toaster.' Vina looked at her condescendingly and proceeded to show her. Then Rani buttered the toast and placed two Marie biscuits in a china plate that was patterned with some strange creatures around the edges. Vina had the tea ready.

The two went into Sadhna's room. Vina entered without knocking and said cheerily, 'Your tea, Didi.'

Sadhna was sitting up with a notebook and a pen. She nodded in silence and pointed to the table beside her. Vina put the tray down and settled herself on the rug there. 'What a hot day it is!' she said, fanning herself with her chunni. Sadhna did not answer. Vina scrutinized Sadhna's face carefully. 'You seem to be turning darker. You should use Dove soap.' Sadhna still refused to answer. Vina casually picked up the television remote control and flicked it on.

A hysterical news anchor started shouting into the room about a recent terrorist attack. 'Uff,' Vina said. 'Idiot!' and changed the channel. Katrina Kaif in a sari and Akshay Kumar in a turban sang to each other in front of the Eygptian pyramids. Vina settled back, her mouth slightly open. Rani, finding both the women ridiculous in different ways, stood motionless in a corner of the room.

Sadhna, still holding her notebook and pen, shut her eyes, looking miserable. The tea, the toast and the Marie biscuits sat desolate, untouched.

Three

Several weeks passed. The days were hot and dusty. Rani's days had settled into a routine. She was given no specific tasks. Rani and Vina shared the cooking, cleaning and other odd jobs between themselves. Rani helped Sadhna hobble with her crutches from one room to another and to the bathroom, Sadhna still being immobile.

Rani sleepwalked through these weeks, her mind either on Bittu or still seething with anger at the way her father had been treated. She had sporadic bursts of energy when she would dust and scrub the house vigorously. At other times, complete lethargy would descend upon her, when she felt her life had no direction or meaning, and she would exasperate Vina by staring into space or chopping vegetables excruciatingly slowly.

Rani had trouble sleeping at night and when she could manage to drift off, she would have recurring nightmares of Ravan burning. Somewhere through the dream, Ravan's face would turn into Papaji's, a sad shrivel. Rani would wake up, her face wet with scalding tears.

✧ ✧ ✧

One Saturday morning, Vina asked for a day off. She had a cousin living in Dakshinpuri who was to get married. Vina wanted to go along for the wedding shopping. She left at 7 am, eyes laden with eyeliner, lashes sticking together with mascara, wearing bright-pink lipstick and a parrot-green salwar-kameez. She left in her wake a strong whiff of heavy perfume. And Rani was left to hold the fort.

At about 11 am, the doorbell rang. Rani opened the door, a little surprised. Sadhna had few visitors. A young woman with kohl-lined eyes and a silver nose ring stood there. Rani gave her a half-smile. But she just looked over Rani's shoulder and said, 'Is Sadhna here? Just go and tell her that it's Sasha.' After saying this Sasha whipped out a cellphone from her bag, punched in a number quickly and began to talk rapidly into it. A little disoriented, Rani went in and repeated the message dutifully to Sadhna, who, as usual, was sitting on the couch, her plastered leg up on the table, a book in her lap and reading glasses perched on her nose. Sadhna immediately panicked at the message. 'No, no,' she said in a sibilant whisper, 'tell her I am out.'

'Your leg is broken,' Rani reminded her respectfully.

'Tell her I am asleep then. Tell her I am dead. Tell her anything. Just don't let her in. She will talk and talk.'

Rani nodded and was about to go back to the door when she saw that Sasha had already let herself in. Sadhna immediately and adroitly changed her groan into a smile.

Sasha was a junior editor at a new weekly that purported to publish nothing but the truth. It had created quite a stir and had all its staff swaggering about all over Delhi.

'Hi dearie, long time,' Sasha said.

Sadhna smiled. 'Hi Sasha, found time away from your parties finally?' she asked, a slight edge to her voice. Oblivious to it, Sasha flopped down on the couch, flinging off her neon-coloured flip-flops and putting her feet up. 'What parties? Just working in that hellhole and then getting wasted in the evenings, partying with morons. I swear I am going on a detox diet. Anyway, how is your little footsie doing?'

'It is better, but it's still a pain.'

'Pity, you are missing a lot of stuff.'

Sadhna stretched her arms over her head. 'I don't think so.'

'And that is why darling, you are where you are. If only you would listen to me. You are lousy at networking.'

Rani came in with a glass of orange juice on a tray. Sasha looked up as if surprised to see her there. 'Oh thanks,' she said enthusiastically.

Then she made a quick birdlike movement with her head and said to Rani, 'This is without sugar, right?"

Rani didn't answer. She didn't know. She looked at Sadhna for instructions.

'Just bring the carton to me,' Sadhna said.

Rani resignedly went back to the refrigerator and took out the carton. In clearly printed words it said, 'No added sugar. Hundred per cent fruit juice.' She went back and repeated this.

Sasha raised her eyebrows at Sadhna.

Sadhna knew by now that Rani had studied till Class Nine. She said a little awkwardly, 'Oh yes, she can read a little.'

'Oh, great!' Sasha gave Rani a dazzling smile. 'Not bad.'

Rani left quietly. The compliment left her fuming. If she had studied a little more, idiotic girls with nose rings and no manners would not be so surprised that she could read.

Sasha tripped into the kitchen five minutes later. She located a bottle of wine and a bottle opener, the broad sleeves of her pink top sweeping spoons and cutlery off the slabs, which she did not seem to notice at all. With another dazzling smile at Rani she left the kitchen, two wine glasses held precariously by their stems.

The two women then called a number and ordered something called a 'risotto', that Rani had never heard of. When she opened the hot carton to serve it to them, she saw messy, overcooked rice. There were also some strange, pasty-looking squares. Doubtfully, Rani scooped out portions in their plates and served them. Sasha grew more boisterous as the afternoon wore on; Sadhna seemed to grow relaxed and thoughtful. All of their conversation was in English, but Rani could grasp some parts of it clearly. At one point she heard Sadhna ask, 'You keep saying it is a "crappy" job. Why do you do it? You are young. It isn't as if you have a family to support or a house to run. You can work hard in any direction you please. This might be a new venture, fresh and honest now, but it will go the same way. It has the same crappy kind of people. And if you don't like them, why do you hang out with them so much?'

Rani wondered what 'crappy' meant. Nothing good, by the sound of it.

Sasha seemed a little taken aback by such direct criticism. 'You are so cynical. And anyways, what else can I do?' she said, sounding defensive. 'How do I fit in? And it's not like there are many great, brilliant people out there. The crappy ones *are* the best, darling,' she finished.

'I don't know. I don't think so. There is always a way. Has to be.'

'Well, you haven't found it either. Have you?'

Sadhna fell silent.

'So forget it,' Sasha said, her confident tone back. 'Here's to today.'

And they clinked their glasses together.

Mad, Rani thought. Compared to them even Bittu seemed sensible.

After a while Sasha came to the point, 'Okay Sadhna, you gotta do me a favour. I need to throw a party and my digs are too small. So can I have one here?'

Before Sadhna could reply, she quickly interjected, 'I will take care of everything. You don't have to do a thing. But it's really important.'

'Important to whom?'

'Well, to me for one. And it could be to you, if you decided to play your cards right.'

'Who will be coming?' Sadhna asked, tiredly ignoring the bit about playing cards.

'Some people, some journo friends, all in senior positions. Hoping to get a couple of biggies too. Something should come out of it.'

'Okay, fine. Do it,' Sadhna said putting her glass down and wishing she had the use of her legs. Then at least you could walk out on people. It wouldn't be possible to do that for quite a while now.

This Sasha woman was giving her a headache, Rani thought. She wondered if she could go to her room. To be on the safe side, she unrolled a chatai on the kitchen floor and lay down there to rest, close enough to hear if they called her. Later, after the strange Sasha had left, Rani happened to glance at the bill that still lay in the kitchen for the 'risotto'! ₹550! Rani stared at the bill unbelievingly. What idiots these women were! And how undeserving! These were the kind of amounts that her father, with his clean kurta, his *Dainik Bhaskar* and his gentle voice had been questioned about, harassed about. And here these women had leftovers on their plates along with crumpled tissues, ready to be emptied into the dustbin. It was barbaric.

In their home, in Amritsar, nobody would dream of throwing away good food. Any leftovers were carefully stored in steel boxes with lids. Rani tore the bill into little bits and wished with great intensity that she could just once visit Amritsar, open the battered refrigerator at home again, heat up aloo bhaji and share it with Bittu in front of the television. Just as she was thinking this indignantly, Sadhna called for her. She told Rani, 'You'll have to throw away the food on her plate. These people don't always think before serving themselves. But the rest you can put in a plastic container. Make sure you cover it and put it in the fridge. You or I can have it later.'

Rani nodded and went to the kitchen to do as she had been told. She felt a little annoyed that Sadhna had not let her continue to feel resentful.

Four

Despite her altered relationship with everything literary, Sadhna had been attempting to write a second novel. It was a novel about a man called Rajendra Dubey, who would contemplate suicide every ten days or so, filling the intervening days by working hard as a schoolteacher at a government school in Dhanbad.

The novel had been in progression for six years now. When Sadhna had written the first one, it had been a private, exciting act. Now, when almost everybody she knew had written at least one novel, the idea did not seem as exciting or revolutionary. However, Sadhna could not stop writing; she had become attached to Rajendra Dubey and almost felt that he was her brother. He had taken on a life of his own. He was sensitive but a little impulsive, given to fits of melancholia. Every now and then, Sadhna had to save him from a perilous, self-inflicted end. However, she could understand his feelings. It was not easy being alone, teaching in a school where neither the students nor the authorities cared about learning. At times, he made her furious with his lack of activity and initiative. Sadhna wrote a bit of Rajendra Dubey's life everyday. A very little bit. But everyday, without fail.

✧ ✧ ✧

Her morning chores done, Rani sat looking out of the living-room window gloomily. She disliked the never-ending roar of the traffic outside.

It whizzed past right through the day and right through the night – trucks, buses, autos, cars – till Rani had visions of the whole of Delhi rushing about in a constant frenzy fuelled entirely by anxieties and desires.

She might get used to it soon, she told herself comfortingly.

One could get used to anything. But she was still unused to the city, and even more so to the posh house she was living in now, in a residential colony where tall iron gates clanged shut on their residents every night, trapping them in air-conditioned, television-ed jails.

The house was huge by Rani's standards. It was a bungalow with a tiny garden in the front, flowerpots lining the drive, many rooms and was pleasantly airy. However, Rani, being used to smaller, cozier places, felt a little unsettled. She continued to watch the steady stream of traffic outside, knowing that the few tatters of peace left in the room would soon be shattered by Vina.

God alone knew how Sadhna handled the household. It dawned upon Rani that all across India, from Delhi to Bangalore, from Patna to Pune, from Allahabad to Trivandrum, women in middle-class households effortlessly kept the proprieties and emotions in their homes balanced, day after day, without struggle. Rani wondered at the national accomplishment.

✧ ✧ ✧

Rani truly disliked living here. Break-ins, robberies and murders were as common in Delhi as rain used to be in Cherrapunji when Rani was a schoolgirl. Now she believed it did not rain as much in Cherrapunji. She wasn't certain but she thought she had heard Papaji mention it once.

Rani was startled by every unexpected sound at night. She would hear the colony watchmen whistle, who intended it to be a reassuring sound, but it would make her claustrophobic. And even during the still afternoons, Rani would find the atmosphere eerie. Rows upon rows of large houses, with lives carefully tucked away inside, when you couldn't hear a thing and when any creak or bang could mean a stranger trying to break in, casually, as if it were all in a day's work.

Rani had tentatively asked Sadhna if she felt afraid living here on her own. Sadhna had just said a simple no. What she did not tell Rani was that she wasn't as afraid of being assaulted or killed as she was by what would follow. Grisly details by hyperventilating newscasters and the words that would spew out of their flushed faces. Woman's skull beaten in. Lone woman murdered and robbed. Thirty-seven-year-old writer stabbed to death. Woman's head bashed in, house looted.

It made Sadhna shudder with distaste.

She could not hope for a sedate newscaster with a well-modulated voice saying in a delicate, dignified manner, 'The life of a stalled novelist was brought to an end with some violence. Quite pointless.'

✧ ✧ ✧

The next week there was a brief but unwelcome intrusion into Rani's more-or-less settled routine.

She was chopping onions while Vina peeled carrots and they were chatting desultorily, when a flashy red car roared up to the gate of the house and screeched to a halt. A woman dressed in white, hair streaked with what Rani knew to be Loreal's 'Hi-Color Hi-lights', and sunglasses pushed up on her forehead got out. She walked in with brisk confidence.

Sadhna was sitting on the living-room sofa, having coffee and reading the *Sunday Times*, wondering at how any organization comprising fairly competent staff could turn out something so completely full of rubbish. Vaishali strode into the living room.

'Hello, Sadhna,' Vaishali said, ignoring Rani completely, miraculously managing to make her voice both acidic and syrupy at the same time.

'Hi, Vaishali. How are you?' Sadhna said, in, Rani felt, a somewhat cool voice.

'The usual. How are *you*?' she asked, walking into the drawing room and flopping down on a sofa with a great show of tiredness. Rani took an instant dislike to her, which Papaji had often asked her not to do.

Without waiting for an answer from Sadhna, Vaishali continued, 'Listen, I tried calling but couldn't get through to your number. I wanted to tell you that Lucky ... you remember Lucky? He's lost his father.' She said it in the same tone as she would have if Lucky had lost his car keys.

Sadhna remembered Lucky, a gawky teenage boy who went to mathematics tuition with her and Vaishali when they were in school together.

Sadhna was silent for a moment. Vaishali suddenly whipped out her cellphone from her handbag and punched in a number. Rani brought her a glass of water on a tray. She took it wordlessly, without a glance towards Rani. Vaishali shouted into the phone, 'Ganga, chop the garlic also. Have you chopped the onions?' Ganga, the unfortunate chopper, said something that made Vaishali shout into her BlackBerry, 'I said – chop the onions *lengthways*. Is it your ears or your brain at fault? Now chop four more.'

Rani itched to slap her but went in to make coffee at a sign from Sadhna.

Vaishali put the phone back into her bag and turned to Sadhna with a martyred air. 'Sorry yaar, you know how these people can drive you up the wall! Anyway, so he passed away a while back and the prayer meeting is today. I know I should have called earlier but you know, what with the children's schools and birthday parties and Akash's office parties and then we had to buy a split AC and get it installed ... You have no idea how much work all this is – husband and children and running a household.'

'How is Lucky?' Sadhna asked quietly.

'Well, okay, I suppose. Must be sad. But life has to go on. Anyways, his wife told me to inform you but it slipped my mind. The prayer meeting is in half an hour. We should go. They are a very influential family. And, I mean, we are sort of his friends, right? Can you get dressed for it in time?'

Sadhna remembered how Lucky used to stare at algebra problems in confusion, as if hoping one day they would all make sense to him. He was always getting into trouble for losing things. He'd turn up without his notebook, his pen, would spend ages after the tuition crawling under the chairs looking for his motorcycle keys, would borrow money because he had lost his last twenty. Sadhna felt melancholic at the thought of him losing his father. Some people seemed to be made for loss.

'Yes, I'll get dressed,' Sadhna said. 'But it will take me a while.'

'No problem. Nice coffee,' she said, still not looking at Rani, who was polishing the glass of one of the windows. 'Listen, do you want to come to the mall with me after it? You know how busy Akash is. I have to pick up jeans for Manav, he outgrows them so fast, and I was thinking, maybe Crocs for myself, my feet hurt so much.'

'I fractured my leg, Vaishali, you didn't notice. It's still healing; I don't think I can go around malls.'

'Oh, I am so sorry!' Vaishali said brightly. 'Does it hurt?'

'Not anymore.'

'Then come, yaar.'

'I still have trouble walking,' Sadhna said, trying to keep her voice controlled.

'Arre Baba, just bring one of your maids with you. And Sadhna, wear something suitable. If not in white, at least in beige or something suitable.'

Sadhna decided to take Rani along. She'd need help, she knew. Rani helped her dress and then went and combed her own hair neatly into a plait.

The three were set to go.

Rani and Sadhna sat in the car with Vaishali, glumly listening to her talk non-stop about credit cards, home loans, weekend river-rafting trips and the best event managers in the city.

She spoke throughout on the way to the hall where the prayer meeting was being held. Sadhna had little inclination to speak. Vaishali did not seem to want to listen much either.

Rani wondered what she was *doing* in this car with these people!

✧ ✧ ✧

Women sat around gracefully, cross-legged or with their legs folded to one side, dressed in white or tasteful pastels. Designer handbags and mobile phones lay by their sides, faithful, silent. A priest sat muttering prayers. All the members of the bereaved family were in white. Sadhna and Vaishali sat down, Rani sitting as close to Sadhna as she could.

Vaishali had magically changed her vivacious expression to a suitably subdued one. Sadhna stared at the priest. He seemed practised, at ease, like a seasoned actor.

Rani could not bear to look at Lucky's father's portrait. She felt an unreasonable affection and empathy for the stranger's framed and garlanded being. Memories of another such picture came rushing back to her. And with those memories came a feeling of suffocation.

Vaishali reached for her phone quietly and discreetly pressed a button. She bowed her head low and held the phone to her ears, cupping it with her palm. She was calling home, Rani knew, because she whispered into the phone, 'Ganga? Is the rogan josh ready?' Rani and Sadhna looked away, vaguely disturbed.

While she tried to hear the answer through the crackling line, the priest prayed for the peace of the departed soul.

Sadhna felt the familiar feeling of nausea come up and groaned inwardly. It was becoming a nuisance.

'And yes,' Vaishali continued, 'marinate the chicken. Just coat it with a mix of ginger-garlic paste and curd and leave it. Okay?' She turned to Sadhna and explained apologetically, 'We are having a dinner party tonight. So tough to coordinate everything.'

The widow shuffled by, accompanied by her daughter, making her way to the ladies' toilet of the community prayer hall. Vaishali hung up quickly and looked soulfully at the red-eyed widow.

Sadhna looked at her too, trying to focus, trying to look sympathetic and failing. Her nausea was worse and her head swam.

Sadhna gave Vaishali a sarcastic, resigned half-smile. Vaishali gave her a puzzled smile back that was a little condescending. These arty-farty people, Vaishali thought, just didn't know how to behave. Imagine smiling at a condolence meeting! Sadhna had been a little strange even in school!

Fans whirred overhead. A kitten outside peered into the prayer hall from a window. A fly settled on the priest's nose and he flicked it away in irritation. Sadhna and Vaishali sat in complete silence for another ten minutes, making and breaking eye contact, actively beginning to find each other more and more absurd.

Sadhna closed her eyes, trying to will the nausea away. Rani sat lost in memories.

Vaishali was making another call now.

'There *are* two new bottles of Jack Daniel's, aren't there?' she was asking anxiously in her low, discreet voice. 'If there aren't, ask the driver to go and buy some. That is why I left him at home. They will be for ₹2700 each.'

Sadhna overheard a woman in an adjoining group say, 'They've hired the best prayer hall. It is ₹5000 per day.'

Then Rani saw Lucky pass some currency notes to the priest.

Dinner parties, death and commerce seemed to be playing Ring a Ring o' Roses here.

Vaishali was running late so Sadhna and Rani took a taxi back home. They were silent for the first five minutes of the journey. Then Sadhna looked at Rani to see a tear steal out of Rani's left eye. Sadhna placed her hand over Rani's. Rani turned to her, her face steely, angry. 'She was … she didn't …' Sadhna nodded and patted Rani's hand again. 'Let it be. That is how life is. That is how people are. Doesn't mean they are evil.'

'I know,' Rani answered.

And they spoke no more during the journey home, staring out of opposite windows.

At a traffic signal, a boy in a tattered T-shirt was selling *Vogue*.

Five

The evening of Sasha's party arrived. Vina and Rani lined up the snacks that Sasha had left for the party on the kitchen counters. She had also left a bewildering array of bottles and fruit juices for mocktails and cocktails, as she cheerfully told Vina and Rani.

'What are they?' Rani asked Vina. 'What *is* she always talking about?'

Vina tapped her forehead with her finger and pointed at Sasha. 'Cracked up, she is. But you should see the car she has,' she said, with unwilling admiration.

Mocktail. Cocktail. Mocktail. Cocktail. The words had a nice ring to them, Rani thought. Then Rani began to make up a story in her head to tell Bittu when she next met him of two brothers called Mocktail and Cocktail, and a villain who wanted to cut their tails off.

Sadhna looked strained all day and in an uncharacteristic confiding moment, murmured to Rani that she really did not enjoy parties. 'Can't see much point in them,' she said in her no-nonsense voice.

Vina heard her and gave her a disapproving look.

Rani found the snacks a little strange. Squares of capsicum and onion were spiked onto mutton and chicken pieces with toothpicks. Rani had never seen snacks like this before and personally found it a silly way to eat. There was an assortment of other snacks that were completely alien to Rani. She thought back to the Sunday mornings when Neelam would make aloo-puri and everyone would sit together to eat. Not a morsel would be left and Bittu would always boast that he could eat more puris than any other boy in the neighbourhood. Bittu would make short work of these snacks, Rani thought.

Sasha arrived before everybody else. Vina gazed adoringly at her streaked, curled, waist-length hair. Sasha threw some colourful rugs down on the drawing-room floor. Out of her car, she dragged in two lamps, 'Mood lighting!' she said brightly to Rani.

Then she came into the kitchen and checked all the snacks. She suddenly began speaking with intelligence and clarity and explained carefully in what order and in which plates the snacks were to be served. There was a serving window between the kitchen and the drawing room so when the first few guests began to filter in, Rani could see them. Vina was busily polishing glasses.

Sadhna sat quietly in her chair, greeting everyone with a slightly sardonic smile. Her leg was still in plaster.

It was quite an informal party. Rani stared curiously at everyone from the kitchen, trying her best to overhear everything. A couple came in, evidently in high spirits. The woman called the man Adi and the man addressed her as Babes. Strange names, Rani thought.

A woman called Shagun, wearing a floral printed dress, followed and draped herself languidly over a sofa. A man with a grey beard in a kurta-pyjama entered and got a lot of attention.

'Pradipto Ghosh. *The* man! Great to see you here,' Shagun said to him, in a loud voice and with a dramatic gesture. Rani assumed that he must be the eldest and to be respected. Sasha greeted everyone brightly with hugs and smiles.

Then came a woman wearing raccoon-like eyeliner, dressed in a Fabindia kurta, a white churidaar and a dozen thin silver bangles. Rani thought she looked inordinately pleased with herself even while doing ordinary things like drinking water or smoothing her hair. Everyone made a big deal of her.

'Nina Chowdhary! How are you? We've been seeing a lot of your name in print!' Pradipto said when she entered.

'Hey, Pradipto!' she said, in a sultry, intelligent voice. 'I have just been working really really hard.'

Then an intense conversation followed between Pradipto and Nina of which Rani could not follow much. 'What we are trying to do is to concentrate on what the mainstream media avoids,' Nina ended, Pradipto looking at her intensely, nodding with a profound look on his face.

The last guest to arrive, after a half hour or so, was a woman in a strappy top and jeans. Rani noticed that she had a scarf tied around her neck. She looked exhausted.

Pradipto raised his eyebrows at her, 'And Antara, what makes you late, darling?' he asked.

Rani, who was arranging more mineral water glasses in a tray, felt puzzled. Fatherly men in kurta-pyjama generally did not say 'darling'. In fact, they frowned upon it.

'I was caught in a traffic jam,' Antara said sullenly, taking off her silk scarf and throwing it down on the sofa.

The bearded man poured himself a glass of wine and offered one to her.

'Oh yes!' Shagun said. 'I saw in the morning news that Gujjars are demonstrating in Delhi today again. Jams all over the city.'

'Well,' Nina Chowdhary said seriously, swilling the wine in her glass, 'we must take the marginalized seriously.'

Rani took another tray, feeling a little tired now. The constant talk was exhausting her mind. Even if she could not follow all of the conversation, she could sense there was no affection, no real camaraderie here. Just clever performances. She placed a few paneer tikkas in a circular arrangement and then spent five minutes amusing herself by dabbing dots of ketchup on each tikka to make two eyes, a nose and a mouth. Each tikka was a wild animal. The lettuce and the greens that had come with the tikkas were strewn around the animals to make a jungle. She took out the magical plates and offered them to the guests. They all smiled and thanked her profusely but nobody noticed the jungle. The talk did not cease for a moment.

Sasha, who had gone to the bathroom to touch up her make-up and brush her tresses, reappeared.

'Why so late?' she asked Antara, having missed the previous conversation.

'Bloody Gujjars!' Antara said succintly, and they poured themselves another glass of wine.

✧ ✧ ✧

Rani saw that Vina had applied lip gloss and was wearing a tasselled yellow dupatta in honour of the party. Rani herself was plainly dressed. Vina was heating some snacks in the microwave, a machine that Rani had still not learnt to use.

Vina nudged Rani, 'Look at them – this is how they dress up for parties! And you will never believe it but dressed like that, some of them even get their pictures printed in the newspaper on the photo page. I have seen them with my own eyes.' Vina looked grudgingly impressed. Rani thought of all the women she had ever helped get dressed and made up for parties and weddings, and had to admit that these people were somewhat unusual. But what did it matter? Everything and everyone puzzled her now.

Sasha came hurrying into the kitchen again and urged Rani to take yet another plate of unidentifiable snacks around. Rani felt awkward serving people this way. In her head, she still wasn't a *servant*. But she took the tray out again and caught fragments of conversations.

Now that a couple of hours had passed, the levels in the bottles had gone down and snack trays had emptied, the conversations seemed to have become longer and more involved. Rani listened, caught in an unfamiliar, surreal world.

'Oh, she is *such* a wannabe. We ought to do a piece on her. Something on the lines of *Main Madhuri Dixit Banna Chahti Hoon*. Get her contact, no?' Nina Chowdhary said animatedly to Sasha. Sasha nodded sagely. 'Excellent idea,' she said. 'Totally fresh approach.'

Vina nudged Rani. 'The earrings that that Nina woman is wearing, I am going to buy a pair like that at the Friday market. And I will buy a packet of bindis,' she continued dreamily, as if there was no party going on, as if there was no work to be done. 'A multi-coloured pack,' she added decisively. 'And nail polish. Will you come with me? Do you want to buy nail polish?' Rani studied her bare, short nails. She had forgotten all about things like nail polish since Papaji had gone. 'I'll see,' she said shortly, trying to keep her voice friendly.

Rani took another plate in. Meanwhile, Antara was saying to Pradipto, 'But that *is* what the Indian novel is like now …' Pradipto replied, his voice deep, passionate, helping himself to some snacks, 'It's all about re-inventing the form. We as a nation are just too immature, unformed. And well, if we can't re-invent it, we must admit that the novel is dead. We need to think fresh. We need to think new.'

Some ants scurried to a crumb he had dropped and, completely ignoring Pradipto, patiently laboured to carry each tiny bit of it back to their homes. When they encountered his chappal-clad feet, a deep, collective sigh went up among them and they re-routed themselves, trudging all the way around the chappals.

Rani stood there, still, watching them.

'We need to imagine the unimaginable,' Pradipto ended.

'Once a person becomes famous as a blogger or a columnist, he or she writes at least one novel with great ease, with very little suffering,' Sadhna interrupted, a little disjointedly, her voice abrupt, slightly edgy.

'Oh, but why must a novelist suffer *at all*?' Nina said, with a light laugh. 'That is such a quaint, romantic notion. The reclusive writer working alone in a garret. I mean, who writes like that anymore?'

'Nobody,' Sadhna replied, her face inscrutable.

And then Sadhna felt her old, familiar problem coming back. In the middle of ordinary days, middle of conversations or at any random moment, she would experience waves of nausea. No doctor had been able to cure her. Sadhna beckoned Rani to her. Rani helped Sadhna to the bathroom when Sadhna calmly, soundlessly threw up, washed her face and patted it dry with a towel. She smiled comfortingly at Rani who looked anxious. 'Nothing to worry about. Happens to me all the time. Just don't mention it to anyone.'

And Rani helped her back into the chittering-chattering party.

✧ ✧ ✧

Adi and Babes were lost in each other, nuzzling and kissing till Rani didn't know where to look. At a sign from Sadhna she went to them, bearing a platter of assorted cheeses. Babes groaned.

'Ooh, the calories! The temptation! Go away. Go away.'

Rani recoiled, alarmed. 'She is just joking,' Sadhna smiled at Rani. Rani was such a funny little thing, Sadhna thought. At this fresh encouragement, Rani gingerly extended the dangerous platter to the couple again. Adi took two pieces, thanked Rani and continued his conversation with Babes, 'Yaar, they shot in Ladakh, it was awesome. We should go there sometime.'

'It is clear to the *meanest* intelligence that he does all those shots in Ladakh just for the awards,' Shagun said confidently to the whole room.

'Oh darling, you always hit the nail on the head!' Sasha said, placing a familiar hand on Shagun's shoulder.

Shagun did not look too pleased. Sasha withdrew her hand.

Pradipto Ghosh was still going on. Like a TV anchor, Rani thought to herself.

Vina couldn't keep her eyes away from the guests, with special attention to Adi and Babes.

'They should all be in cages,' she whispered to Rani. 'All zoo type. No?'

Rani smiled, slightly worried about the calm, effortless way Sadhna had thrown up.

Pradipto Ghosh's cellphone rang. 'Hi there,' he said, then listened carefully for a while. 'But don't you know? He has moved to O&M now. Am at a get-together right now. Will call later.'

Rani wondered what O and M was.

Rani was beginning to get a headache. She could make no head or tail of all the talk. She was feeling cross now. When *would* this crowd leave?

Rani had noticed that Sadhna, though a smiling hostess, had not really spoken much. She beckoned Rani to her, after a few minutes. When Rani went over, she said, 'Why don't you and Vina have a cup of tea. And some snacks if you want.'

Rani nodded, grateful for the break. As she left the room, she heard Antara say, 'I am dying for a cigarette now.'

'Idiot!' Rani thought irrationally.

✧ ✧ ✧

Sadhna replayed the evening in her head after the last guest had left. Sasha had stayed back to clear up. The guests had, in all sincerity, talked about art, meaning, experimentation and truth. And equally sincerely, they had spoken of stories of success, networking, awards, big deals and huge advances. Sadhna felt a little false, a little contaminated after the evening. Was she letting Rajendra Dubey down?

Meanwhile, Sasha leaned back contentedly. 'Quite successful, wasn't it? Even though Antara remains peevish, even after several drinks. Good alcohol is wasted on that woman.'

Sadhna sat leaning back too, her eyes closed, silent.

Rani came up to Sadhna holding a pair of earrings made of engraved peacock-blue stone. She held them out to Sadhna and said, 'Didi, I think Babes Madam left these here?'

Sadhna laughed her first real laugh of the evening. 'Her name is not Babes, Rani. It is Gayatri. Only Adi calls her 'Babes'. Out of affection, you see.' Rani did not see, but was too tired to try or even care. She handed the earrings to Sadhna, fetched a broom and began sweeping the floor. Educated people, were they, she thought angrily. And yet they were as bad as the boys in the streets at home when it came to littering.

Sasha suddenly spoke up again, 'Wasn't it great to get Pradipto Ghosh at one of our parties? His is a new publishing house but *really* happening. And the best part is, with all my Sasha-style meticulous planning, I spent only 18,500 on the party. Including the booze,' Sasha said triumphantly, looking completely content.

Rani froze mid-movement.

₹18,500 was the exact, the precise amount that had been spent when their home had been flooded.

Had Papaji had that amount, he would have escaped untold suffering.

Rani's mind could not even respond to the thought.

It was unbearable.

Such a joke.

She felt an intense hatred surge in her heart, a heart which had hardly known hatred before.

A hatred for Sadhna, for Sasha and for all the guests who had drifted in casually, relaxed, chatted and left, with no inkling of the dark rooms that souls could get lost in, for as trivial reasons as a bill of ₹18,500.

Six

The anger did not leave Rani or abate even slightly in the days that followed. The one single thought of that bill followed her all the time. 18,500. 18,500. 18,500. It became a constant refrain in her head. It made her hate everyone, and with it came the misery that only hatred can bring.

Also, though she did not like to admit it to herself, Rani missed Amritsar, and what she still secretly thought of as 'home'. She missed lying on the charpai in the sun, with Bittu cracking peanuts nearby. She missed the hum of the old bazaar outside where you could step out from your house straight into a world of normal people, chaat stalls, the paanwala's radio blaring out film songs, children sailing paper boats in the dirty drains outside and the comforting din of the stall owners shouting out their wares.

It had been more than a month since Rani had come to Delhi. And she hadn't heard a word from Neelam or Mahesh, though she knew that they could have asked Seema for her address. This pinched at her heart a little but not enough to hurt. Then, one afternoon, when the post came, there was a blue inland letter for her. Vina was curious but Rani ran off to her room with the letter wordlessly. With trembling hands, she opened it.

It was from Seema, written so incoherently, mostly in Hindi, with a few misspelt words interspersed in English, that only someone who had grown up with Seema could comprehend it. Seema had first written horizontally saying that she hoped Rani was happy and that Satish, unable to take the parting from her, had grown thinner and paler. This was followed by 'ha ha' written about fourteen times, widely spaced. Then, apparently realizing that she would run out of space, Seema had continued in minuscule handwriting that Rani had to strain to read. She had steered away from all topics that she thought might upset Rani. There was no mention of Mahesh and Neelam and none at all of Dheeraj. She informed Rani that her bhabhis were harassing her because she practised dancing to '*Dhoom tananana*' from *Om Shanti Om* every evening. But she persisted with the dancing because, as she explained, 'All wise people say that perseverance is a virtue'.

Then Seema had run out of space, had turned the sheet of paper at right angles and had continued to write in the margins. She said that Kavita had visited her to ask for Rani's address. She was married and wanted to send Rani a photograph of herself with her husband. She had left happily after noting down the address, smilingly telling Seema that her mother-in-law was a sorceress and a witch. Seema ended the letter by saying again that she hoped that Rani was happy and that there was a good-looking electrician close to where she lived, hopefully with a strong resemblance to Satish. The letter ended abruptly without Seema signing off.

The letter warmed Rani's insides, making her feel that she was not totally friendless and alone in the world, and she cheered up visibly, even deigning to be friendly with Vina.

✧ ✧ ✧

Sadhna's plaster was finally off. But she still used crutches to hobble around. One afternoon, Vina was working in the kitchen and Rani was cleaning the living room. Sadhna sat staring at the intricate blue-and-yellow floral pattern on the window curtains that cut off the blinding sunlight from outside, turning it gentler. She had been scribbling at her wretched novel again. Rajendra Dubey was falling in love with another schoolteacher, a pretty, mild-mannered colleague who wore simple but pretty cotton saris. So things were happier. From her own experience, Sadhna knew that it was only a matter of time before disillusionment would set in. But meanwhile, she'd let Rajendra Dubey be happy and live life as it should be lived. She closed her notebook with a sigh.

'Can you read well, Rani? Or just a little bit?' Sadhna asked her as Rani diligently scrubbed a spot on the otherwise shining floor. After all, the girl *had* studied till Class Nine. Rani was responsive and friendly enough, but did not volunteer too much of her thoughts or ideas.

'Oh yes, quite a bit,' Rani answered casually.

'And what do you like to read?' Sadhna asked.

'*Filmfare*, mostly. But I haven't read it for a long time now.'

'Why not?' Sadhna asked.

Rani's memory flashed back to that cold, lonely train journey where at several stops she had seen *Filmfare* on magazine stands. And had wondered at the carefree creature she had been, reading these magazines diligently from cover to cover every month.

Everything about that journey seemed surreal.

Carefully thrusting back all thoughts of the journey, of Amritsar, of Papaji and of Bittu, Rani replied, 'Oh, just like that.'

'Um,' Sadhna began hesitantly, 'I could get *Filmfare* for you but don't you find it a little ... um ... repetitive and, well ... nonsensical?'

'Oh yes,' Rani said airily. 'But everything is.'

'Everything is what?' Sadhna asked.

'Repetitive and nonsensical,' Rani said. 'Even newspapers. Murders and accidents, and fat politicians lying and smiling. At least *Filmfare* has Shahrukh.'

'You have a point. I wish I read just *Filmfare* too,' Sadhna said meditatively. 'Apart from books, that is. There is not much point in reading newspapers and magazines these days. All the same. Sheep!' she said disparagingly, looking disheartened.

Rani said comfortingly, 'But most newspapers also have a few separate pages for Shahrukh and the others.'

'That *is* the problem, Rani. Shahrukh should live in *Filmfare* and real people should live in newspapers.'

'Shahrukh *is* real,' Rani said, a little offended. The spot on the floor had disappeared now. Rani, afraid that her tone had been insubordinate, asked politely, 'Can I get you some tea, or coffee?'

Sadhna refused and groaned inwardly. Just as the conversation was becoming interesting, Rani had withdrawn again.

✧ ✧ ✧

Rani, like Vina, was allowed to sit in the living room and watch television. One afternoon, she sat there shelling peas and flicking channels.

One channel had a loud woman with short hair interviewing a crowd of people who did not shut up long enough to hear what the others were saying. When the woman would have had enough of them, she would turn towards the camera and say something to wrap things up then ask another question, beginning another pointless frenzy of opinions.

Rani changed the channel. A man who had started out as a yoga teacher on television was now talking about a political party he was planning to float, advocating the death sentence for all forms of corruption.

Another click, and two slim girls were agonizing over their oily skin. Then, as can only happen in advertisements, they abruptly found a magic product, their oily skin was gone and their lives became perfect.

Rani began to feel unreal and floaty. But she continued to flick channels. An astrologer wearing numerous rings was advising a housewife from Lucknow over the phone to wear an emerald in a ring and feed cows and black dogs to solve all her problems. A dying Amitabh Bachchan reassuringly died in a weeping Nirupa Roy's lap on a movie channel. But when Rani went on to another channel, Amitabh Bachchan betrayed her by appearing at an awards function with his perfect family, Aishwarya Rai glowing, Amar Singh by their side. Rani then watched Jerry eternally tormenting Tom, this time dubbed in Hindi. A ghoulish news anchor described in gruesome detail the murder of an entire family in Gurgaon with visible relish. Rakhi Sawant told an interviewer rapidly that she was Jesus's special child. Shahrukh Khan was telling men that they could now stop swiping women's fairness creams because they had their own now – Fair and Handsome.

Rani felt that at every click of the button, a new monster raised its head. There was a stack of newspapers by her side – still, motionless siblings of the moving monsters on TV.

Cars honked outside.

Rani wanted to run away.

✧ ✧ ✧

The next week, Rani received *two* letters in one afternoon. She was delighted. Both were addressed in Seema's handwriting. Rani eagerly opened the first. In it, Seema had written only two lines. She explained that Bittu had badgered her that he wanted to write to Rani Bua. So Seema had bought him an inland letter, promising to seal, address and post it after he had written it. Bittu's letter followed below. Bittu had written:

> It is very hot.
> It is summer vacation.
> When are you coming back?
> The brown dog in front of Nathu's Sweets has had six puppies.
> Karan fell from the cycle.
> It was his own fault.
> Blood came out of his nose.
> Come home.

Below this missive, he had drawn a neat, recognizable diagram of an air conditioner, clearly copied out of one of the manuals that he often borrowed from Satish. Rani cried over the letter till the air conditioner was damp.

When Rani opened the second letter from Seema, she saw that it was a short one. Seema had just written to tell her that there had been a family fight in Kavita's home, involving the couple, the mother-in-law, two sisters-in-law and a few visiting relatives. Angry, Kavita's husband had struck her on the head with a metal flower vase. Kavita had died on the spot. The matter had been hushed up.

Rani wondered where everything ended.

✧ ✧ ✧

A week later, Rani received another letter, this time in a large envelope.

Kavita had sent it and it had been evidently been delayed in the post. Rani remembered when she slit the envelope open that Kavita had promised to send her either a wedding picture or a post-wedding 'romantic couple picture', as she had called it.

And now that the picture had reached Rani, it was too late. By this time Kavita was dead, from a blow to her head by her husband. In the picture, though, which was a formal one taken in a studio, he looked thin, meek, quiet. Kavita smiled confidently. She was wearing a sequined, maroon, badly-stitched Anarkali kurta. He had an arm around her. There was a vase of pink plastic roses by them and on the wooden background was a beautiful painted pond.

With lotus flowers floating in it.

Seven

One hot, airless day, Rani woke up feeling breathless. She flung the window to their room open. They had to keep it closed at night to keep the mosquitoes out. But no fresh morning air came wafting in. The day was dead, still.

Vina was still asleep. She had ignored all of Rani's advice about removing make-up before going to bed and then moisturizing her face. Vina's face was blotchy with stale blusher, her lipstick was smudged and her eyeliner had flaked off in bits. She looked completely serene.

Rani took a large handkerchief, her father's, and dampened it. She lay back on the bed again with the handkerchief spread over her dry, hot face. It cooled her aching eyes and softened her parched lips.

Certain memories came thundering back into her mind. Familiar voices, smells, sights ... she pushed them all away firmly. She had to remember that she was alone now.

After a while, Rani got up. It was still too early to go downstairs. She took a bath and got dressed but it was still too early. Rani opened her suitcase and idly took out her Shahrukh Khan album that she had brought with her. She leafed through it, looking at his various pictures. And then, she felt a stab of anger at him. What did he know? That her father had died, that she had had to leave home, that she had been separated from her beloved Bittu. Rani looked deep into his melting brown eyes, hoping to feel loved again. But she just saw indifference there. Indifference that she should have seen years ago.

Rani then decided to go down and clean the sink outside the kitchen. She walked softly so as not to disturb the still sleeping Sadhna. She put some Tide powder in a mug, grabbed a nylon scrubber and went to the sink. She had just begun when she glanced up into the mirror over the sink. There was downy hair on the area above her upper lip, her eyebrows were bushy, there were blackheads on her nose and the skin of her face looked rough. She looked like a maidservant, which she was. And her heart seemed to be loaded down by rocks. She could not remember the careless, frivolous girl who had once giggled over silly things with Seema. That girl was nice, Rani reflected casually, as if thinking of a stranger she had met briefly.

And she thought of Papaji, and his gentle admonitions about finishing school. Rani let go the scrubber and the mug, held the stainless steel tap with both hands, bent her head and wept. She wept and wept till her face looked uglier, her skin became blotchy and the vague ache in her temples escalated into a volcanic headache. Her whole life stretched out in front of her which she would spend looking into mirrors in other people's homes, always to find an unkempt, clueless stranger staring back at her. Rani did not know for how long she stood there. She did not know how much time passed before she lifted her bowed head again. Directly in front of her, a lizard had crawled onto the mirror and stationed itself on the exact spot where her nose was. Rani shrieked and sprinted away. She started her work in the kitchen earlier than she was required to. A pile of dirty dishes from yesterday stared at her from the sink. Rani thought nostalgically of a few customers who had always insisted on her threading their eyebrows because they believed she did a fine job.

Rani felt that her skills were being wasted. And she had to be more street-smart. She had to survive. Had Papaji been more street-smart he would have more successful than his contemporaries too, she thought. Rani picked up the bottle of Pril liquid cleaner and the Scotch-Brite scrubber, turned on the sink tap and attacked.

The turbulence in Rani's mind was echoed by the steel utensils that she was soaping, scrubbing, rinsing and attacking ruthlessly, with quick, angry movements. A pulse pounded in her temple. There were loud clanging noises in the kitchen and in her head.

And Vina chose this very day to be exceptionally garrulous. She came down a little late, her eyeliner and new pink earrings already in place, looking fresh and pleased with herself. Rani wanted to throw a jug at her. But then Sadhna woke up, and the two girls busied themselves over her toilette and breakfast.

Not only was the day airless, Rani had a weird cold. She did not sneeze and neither did her nose run. Her nose was just blocked and stuffy. A bead of perspiration formed in the middle of her forehead then trickled gracefully on to the tip of her nose. There was a fan in the kitchen, but it couldn't be switched on while anything was cooking on the stove. Vina was boiling double-toned milk, poured out of Mother Dairy pouches, spilling a good amount on the gas stove as she usually did.

Rani looked at her disdainfully. She wished Vina could work under Asha at Eve's Beauty Parlour for a few days. That might teach her to be more tidy, efficient and, if not normal, at least close to it.

Rani consciously tried to keep her temper in check. She could not understand why she was feeling like this. She rarely got into a temper. Something was wrong with her today. Papaji did not like people losing their temper.

Vina smoothed her hair and said, 'How do you like my new salwar-kameez? I bought it from Madangiri. I also got my eyebrows done. You should take better care of your looks. You are quite pretty otherwise.'

Rani retained a stony silence, wiping the kitchen slab with a dry cloth.

Vina giggled. 'If you are not careful, you will end up like Memsaab or Didi or whatever.'

'What do you mean?' Rani asked her sharply, her voice a little strange because of the stuffy nose.

'See,' Vina said, turning to her with an air of wisdom. 'She lives in a big house, right? Rented or her own, or whatever. But she does live in a big house. Right?'

Rani nodded mutely.

'She has servants, money and all, right?'

Another nod.

'And just *look* at her. Even with the fracture. Look at the way she dresses: no make-up, no colour, no jewellery – gold or silver – absolutely *nothing* to show for anything in her purse.' Vina's voice dripped with contempt.

'She seems to have no inclination to get married, she hardly watches television, just doesn't seem to know how to enjoy life. She has a landline *and* a cellphone but doesn't talk to friends. She just sits stupidly looking out of the window or reading books endlessly. Or else she is writing things in a notebook all day. As if she were keeping accounts for the whole of India. Now if I were in her place, I would do full make-up every morning. Agreed, she can't go to a beauty parlour but in these colonies you can call beauticians home.'

Rani felt a momentary pang at the mention of a beauty parlour. Vina continued, 'I would sit with the air conditioner on each day getting facials and massages, I would eat chicken curry and shahi paneer everyday and watch at least one film every evening. She is impossible. Some people don't know when they are lucky. To look at her, you would think she just came back from a cremation.' As Vina's chatter grew, the movements of her hands slackened. She still hadn't properly cleaned the sticky gas stove on which she had spilt the milk.

'She is very kind to you, you know,' Rani said to Vina, trying to sound reasonable, trying to keep the reproach that she felt out of her voice. 'And to me,' she added.

'All that is true,' said Vina carelessly, 'but she should also behave according to her social standing.'

Rani impatiently took over and Vina stretched her arms, blissfully unaware of the volcanic feelings that threatened to erupt from Rani any moment.

'Life is not the same for everyone,' Rani finally said, in an attempt at calmness. 'Things change. People change, circumstances change. All of us have to live the best way we can.'

'That is true,' Vina said philosophically. 'What can one do? Things change. Even Kareena broke up with Shahid. Who would have thought that could have happened?'

Rani looked at her blankly. Then she remembered some of Kavita's talk. 'Oh, Kareena Kapoor, you mean? The actress?'

'How many other other Kareenas are there? I do mean Kareena Kapoor.' Vina shook the spoons dry in a bunch and began sticking them in their holder one by one. As an afterthought, she added, 'Shahid is also a Kapoor. Mostly,' she continued knowledgeably, 'many successful people are Kapoors. And it is not only them. Even Deepika broke off with Ranbir, though neither of them will admit it. At least not clearly. It's a pity – Deepika could have married Ranbir and become a Kapoor.'

Rani was completely flummoxed. 'When I said that things, people, circumstances change, I meant change in other ways. The way you think, the way you handle problems, the adjustments that are required and you have to change when you lose too many things,' Rani said, speaking more to herself than Vina. Once more, Rani thought, just once more, let me see Papaji's face, hear his voice and I will never ask God for anything else ever again.

'I know,' Vina said, hardly having listened to Rani. 'Who would have thought it of Kareena? But, you know, she is with Saif Ali Khan now. She has beauty, money and fame already. Now she wants to be royalty too.'

Rani stared blankly at Vina. And then at the strange kitchen around her, the unfamilar objects that meant nothing to her.

'I am sick of you,' she suddenly said to Vina, almost conversationally. 'Completely sick.' Vina looked back, no understanding on her face. Then Rani's voice rose slightly.

'I am sick of you – sick, sick, sick.' Rani knew not the source from where the unfamiliar voice arose, threatening to turn itself into a shout at any moment. 'And of your endless clothes and make-up and your stupid, *stupid* eyebrows. And your endless *talk*.' Kavita had also talked a lot, Rani thought, but it had never made Rani angry. What was happening to her now?

Vina stared at her, shocked, immobile, not an eyebrow twitching.

'And I am sick of your Kareena. Day and night Kareena, Kareena, *Kareena*. Never Kareena Kapoor, but Kareena, as if she were your childhood friend. Pretending as if she is not someone who employs hundreds like you to clean her *drains*!' Rani was shouting hysterically now, all the pent-up energy of the past few months flooding out. 'You have *no* idea, no idea of anything. Your head is just full of nonsense and you let it out of your mouth day and night till a person begins to go mad.'

Rani was red-faced now, her forehead and palms sweating. Hot on the forehead and cold on the palms.

Finally, anger began to stir on Vina's face.

'What ...' she began, stepping forward, but Rani was out of control now. The frivolous words spoken by the other girl ceaselessly over the past two months while unspoken grief festered in her own heart had together accumulated in Rani's system like a dangerous cancer. Pus had broken out.

Vina tried to speak, angry and indignant. But Rani wouldn't let her. She brought her face alarmingly close to Vina's and said, 'Stop. Just stop. Just don't speak. Don't speak. I am warning you. Don't speak.'

Rani was shaking now.

This was how Sadhna found them – standing in the kitchen, Rani trembling with rage and fullness. Sadhna had heard every single word of their conversation as for a change she had sat at the dining table outside the kitchen, reading Munshi Premchand's *Godaan*. She had hobbled over to the kitchen with the stick she now used instead of the crutch. Vina looked angry, but at the sight of Sadhna burst into tears.

Then, before Sadhna could intervene, Vina spoke to Rani, finally retorting to the taunt about Kareena, spite gleaming like a coiled snake on her pretty face.

'If Kareena employs hundreds like me to clean her drains, she also must employ thousands like you!'

The three women stood absurdly in the kitchen. Sadhna knew she had to make peace but did not know how to. She placed a hand over Rani's, but Rani shook it away angrily. Her usual equanimity had completely deserted her.

'Look, you both need to calm down now,' Sadhna began.

'I was all calm,' Vina said tearfully. 'This one just started off on me for no reason.'

Sadhna gave Vina a cold look.

'As far as I remember, you were not saying very pleasant things either. Not only were they not pleasant, they were not in the least bit sensible. Go to your room, wash your face and blow your nose,' she said authoritatively. 'And don't come down till I call you.'

Vina paid no attention and continued with her complaints till Sadhna had repeated the order thrice, each time in a firmer voice than before. Vina finally left, making sniffing noises.

Then Sadhna turned to Rani, 'Look, Rani,' she said.

'Oh no,' Rani said, her voice still full of rage. 'You think you will lecture the poor, uneducated maid. To think that *you*, of all people, have any wisdom to give me,' she said derisively.

Sadhna bristled at the sudden personal attack.

'And why am I the last person who should give you advice?'

'Just mind your own business,' Rani said rudely.

Sadhna felt furious. 'And I thought you were the polite one with gentler sensibilities.'

'I don't need a character certificate from you,' Rani snapped. 'People like you don't even know anything.'

'Meaning?' Sadhna asked acidly.

'Meaning, do you even know what 18,500 rupees mean? The kind you just spend on parties. Do you even know what is what? You live in some dream world and just because you can read and write, you think you can bestow wisdom upon any human being. If we had had 18,500, Papaji might have been alive today. I might have been living with Bittu happily instead of living in this miserable hellhole where all you see and hear is traffic. I used to tell him stories. But these days, I sometimes can't even think of one no matter how hard I try.'

Sadhna and Rani were both trembling with anger now.

As if they were in a melodramatic school play where the teacher had given them no instructions about restrained, understated acting.

'And don't I live in the same miserable hellhole?' Sadhna asked Rani quietly. 'Do *I* see anything else but traffic? I, too, loved telling stories, but they just won't come now.' Rani was perplexed for a moment. Then she said in irritation, 'What's the problem with women like you? You have everything done for you. You ought to spend a few days scrubbing the tubs for pedicures and manicures. Then you'd know! You want to go out, you call for a taxi. You want to eat, you telephone for food. You have a comfortable life. And yet you mope around the house, enjoying nothing, as if you were a tragic figure.'

Sadhna gave a sardonic laugh.

'And do you think I can telephone for happiness and they will deliver it at my doorstep?' Sadhna was shaking now. 'So I am sorry if I am richer or at least better off. But I have my own demons so don't give me the tragedy-queen bit.'

'I have a nephew I miss terribly. I love him more than my life,' Rani said.

'I'll never be able to finish this novel and I am sick of it,' Sadhna said.

And then both burst into tears, unable to keep up with each other's stories.

Even completely crazed, each of them had the space in their heads to be relieved that Vina had left and had not witnessed the scene.

Eight

Rani and Sadhna had never in their memories shouted their woes out like this. The next morning, when they met each other's eyes, they felt slightly ashamed. They behaved with complete normality and decorum, though, as if nothing had happened. Rani brought Sadhna her tea, Sadhna thanked her and remarked that the weather seemed a little cooler today. Rani agreed with her. They treated each other with ridiculously elaborate courtesy.

Inside, each felt that they had let the other witness the insane side of their souls. It made them uncomfortable though strangely, also considerably lighter and happier.

They spoke little after this, but in the following weeks, an unstated sympathy developed between them. The earlier hostility and wariness had vanished completely with the outburst.

They felt at harmony with each other. And something, perhaps clogged up stories and emotions, unblocked inside both the women.

That morning, for the first time in days, Sadhna managed to write without going blank, able to find the right words for everything.

While she was writing downstairs, Rani stood on the terrace pegging up the laundry on the clothesline, watching a yellow kite soar high in the sky. The sun was scorching, she thought. The child who was flying the kite should not be doing it. He could get sunstroke. But he had probably sneaked up to the terrace like Bittu while his family imagined him asleep. There must be millions of scamps like Bittu in the country.

Rani smiled up at the big yellow kite dancing against the clear blue sky. Far above it, an eagle soared serenely.

Downstairs, Sadhna finished writing a particularly difficult chapter.

The day became happier.

✧ ✧ ✧

'We are all trapped in urban landscapes, in debt, in a society fast giving itself over to money-loving philistinism,' Sadhna said reflectively to Rani. The two sat together in companionable silence, Sadhna scribbling in her notebook, Rani darning a sari of Sadhna's.

Rani asked wonderingly, 'Does *anyone* understand what you speak?'

'They understand the words but I don't know if they feel it,' Sadhna answered, melancholically. 'It gets so lonely. And Rani, though you say you don't understand the words, I have a feeling that you get it.'

Rani looked a little confused but then said indulgently, 'God alone knows what you are saying. I certainly feel nothing of that sort. But you can think that if it makes you happy.'

There was silence in the room for a while and then Rani said, 'Tell you what, all this thinking is making you pale. Papaji said that too much talk of wisdom can stop a person from living wisely.'

Then Rani stopped abruptly, not wishing to get into a conversation about Papaji.

There was another silence in the room and then Rani suggested hesitantly, 'Would you like me teach you embroidery? I am quite good at it and maybe, if I taught you some new stitches, you would like it.'

'Rani, I don't even know any old stitches. I only believed in learning sensible, useful things. So I can sew on buttons, repair frayed edges, hem and darn. That's it!'

Rani said dreamily, 'Embroidery gets boring if you keep making roses in cross-stitch on silly cushion covers. But if you can think up patterns out of your head and put them down as you please on pleasant cloth, you feel very happy. I just never got enough time to do it.'

Sadhna smiled, 'By the sound of it, you have done enough of it. Tell me more about your work.'

And then, blushing, Rani, for the first time, began to relate to Sadhna the details of her work at Eve's Beauty Parlour, also relating anecdotes.

Sadhna was impressed. 'Really! And you never told me half of this. What exactly did you do there?'

Rani answered with shy confidence, 'Everything.'

She looked at Sadhna and said, 'I started off with threading and pedicures but then I learnt every single thing. Right from draping bridal saris to the most elaborate hairstyles. I could do everything. Papaji said that you should be the best at whatever you do.'

'You miss your Papaji very much, don't you, Rani?' Sadhna asked. Rani tried to hold them back, but the hot tears came gushing out.

Sadhna was dismayed. 'I am sorry. Don't get upset.'

Rani's tears went on for another five minutes. Then she hesitantly, quietly began to tell Sadhna everything. She needed to tell someone. About home, Seema, Eve's Beauty Parlour, Kavita, Bittu, the water pipes, the mourning, the lonely train journey to New Delhi. Everything.

After the quiet narrative stopped, Sadhna beckoned Rani to herself since she couldn't bend easily, and hugged the thin, lonely frame close. Everything else fell away. She wiped Rani's tears and kissed her forehead while her own tears flowed freely.

'I can understand. To see someone you love die, I know ...'

Rani sat up, wiping her tears. She gave Sadhna a wan smile. 'I am behaving like those stupid girls who are always crying.'

'So am I, then,' Sadhna said, smiling too.

Complete understanding passed between the two women. The burdens of two hearts had suddenly become lighter. Love, an oft-repeated and misused word, had finally worked in one of its rarer forms, bringing relief and coolness to two people, even though temporarily.

✧ ✧ ✧

The house became a much happier place. Both Sadhna and Rani became nicer to Vina. Rani apologized to her and Vina accepted, though a little stiffly. There was more laughter in the house

Rani told Sadhna a good deal about Bittu. Sadhna loved hearing about him.

'You said you told him stories at bedtime. Do you remember any?'

Rani answered, a little shyly, 'Most of them are just made up as I went along. But some Bittu would grow to like for some reason. And then he'd want me to repeat those.'

'Tell me some of those,' clamoured Sadhna.

'Forget those stories,' she said. 'They make no sense. Besides, it's easier to start stories than to end them. You won't understand.'

Sadhna laughed out loud.

'Believe me, I understand much much better than you can imagine. In fact, it is not that easy to start stories either. Come on, Rani. Tell me a story now.'

Vina passed, carrying a basketful of tomatoes. Sadhna called out to her, 'Vina, where are you going?'

'To the kitchen to chop tomatoes.'

'Bring the knife and the tomatoes here,' Sadhna said. 'You can chop them here. Rani is going to tell us a story.'

Feeling pleased, Vina settled herself by Rani with about a dozen tomatoes. '₹20 a kilo,' Vina said aloud. Both Sadhna and Rani nodded in empathy.

'Story now,' Sadhna said.

Rani focused at a vague point in the air and began. She could never tell a story if she was making direct eye contact with anyone. She decided to tell one of Bittu's favourite stories. She had never known why it was a favourite with him. It had no battles or high adventure in it.

'Once there was an old neem tree. The leaves were bitter but they were respected greatly by humans. They were supposed to have medicinal properties. The neem tree was in the centre of a village. When children would get rashes and their skin would get itchy, mothers would pluck off leaves from this tree, grind them into a paste and apply them to the affected areas. The children would be soothed. People would boil the leaves in water and mix it with their bath water to keep illnesses away. Even though Colgate toothpaste and brushes had arrived in the small general store in the village, many people still preferred the datun, rubbing their teeth with the twigs of the neem tree till their teeth shone and their mouths smelt fresh.

Then the strangest thing began to happen – the leaves began to grow jealous of each other. Each tiny leaf wished to be the only one with special properties. The twigs, who were usually more sensible, with a slightly more mature approach to life, also began to fall into this trap. Everyone in the tree grew jealous. A crow couple had come to build a nest in this tree. They had just finished building it, and the lady crow was readying to lay the eggs. She complained to her husband, "There is too much jealousy and quarreling in this tree, can't we go and live elsewhere?" The crow answered absentmindedly, "What do you have to do with all of that? They are leaves and twigs, we are birds – just ignore them."

"Yes, but still," she said. "A mother needs a good, positive atmosphere."

"Just relax. Stop talking like humans," her husband told her.

"You should hear yourself sometimes," she said derisively.

And they let it go at that.

Every other day there'd be fights – between leaves from the same branch, between groups of leaves from different branches, between the leaves and the twigs.'

Here Rani stopped smiling, remembering what Bittu had said at this point in the story. 'Just like our mohalla, no, Rani Bua?'

Then she continued.

'One day the crow tried to make peace between everyone. But they called him a mere bird and told him to mind his own business. His wife had laid the eggs now and was blind and deaf to the rest of the world, living in a happy bubble of her own. Eggs had to be the most beautiful things in the world, she thought to herself.

"I tried speaking to the tree trunk," her husband told her. "But the fellow seems immune to everything. Said he'd been here a long time. But that the leaves would come and go. They did as they pleased and he couldn't be bothered with what they said and did." The crow's wife was hardly listening, dreaming of tiny crow babies, happier than she had ever been her entire life, also a little apprehensive. She would protect them from every predator, she thought fiercely.

"Are you even listening?" the crow asked.

"Oh yes," she said, smiling sweetly at him. As much as crows could smile.'

Then Rani faltered. Sadhna and Vina looked at her expectantly.

'What happens next?' Sadhna asked.

Rani looked evasive. 'I don't exactly know,' she said, 'because mostly, at this point, Bittu would already be asleep.'

'Also,' Rani added, 'what *can* happen now?'

Vina looked derisive. And Sadhna looked at Rani, her heart full of gratitude. It was ages since she had felt fresh and young, and uncynical. At least tonight, Rajendra Dubey wouldn't try to kill himself. Sadhna felt hope again.

✧ ✧ ✧

The monsoon had arrived again and made Rani a little homesick. She pictured the familiar dilapidated house with its leaks and swollen wooden windows. She missed Bittu so much on some days that it seemed like a physical ache.

Rani began to ask around for vacancies in good beauty parlours. She had told Sadhna about it; she did not want to do it on the sly. On her way to the market to buy vegetables, on her trips to the chemist and while she ran various errands, she lost no oppurtunity in talking to people, making enquiries. But the answers were not encouraging so far. Some parlours were too far off, others sounded shady. Rani longed to be in a beauty parlour again, hearing the buzz of hairdryers, the familiar feel of the nylon thread twisted around her fingers and the smell of hot wax, face creams and chemical bleach in the air. She left Sadhna's landline number with numerous people, asking them to call if they knew of a vacancy.

Sadhna's leg had almost healed now. She could walk without crutches but still needed the support of a stick. She was not supposed to run, walk over uneven ground or climb stairs. Rani had energized her, taking her fatigue away. She continued to work on her novel. Rajendra Dubey's suicide attempts became less frequent and, in one chapter, he actually confronted the authorities about the lack of sanitation in the school toilets.

Nine

One evening Sasha turned up at Sadhna's doorstep, accompanied by a girl in her mid-twenties. She introduced her as Dia, a graduate from NID with a diploma in Film and Video Communication.

Sadhna was getting tired of Sasha turning up without calling and by her dazzling smile that was supposed to be endearing. But she welcomed the two inside. Vina was quick to make them comfortable and offer them water. Lately, Vina had sensed Sadhna's increasing preference for Rani and was actively working to retain her own number-one position in the household. Dia wore glasses with thick red frames and looked at Sadhna with serious eyes.

'Sasha has told me so much about you,' she said, just a little short of gushing.

'So what exactly is it that you do?'

Sadhna did not know how to answer this. The arty and literary world only knew her through her single published novel. She remained obscure and yet, for some unknown reason, she seemed to have acquired an aura that attracted these people to her.

'Nothing much,' she answered. 'Just a bit of this and that.' Even to herself, her answer sounded irritating and frivolous.

Rani brought in sugar-free orange juice and Sadhna smiled at her.

'You know, Rani tells wonderful stories,' Sasha beamingly told Dia.

Vina scowled. Sadhna regretted having mentioned this to Sasha in an unguarded moment. Now she would give Rani no peace.

Dia studied her glass of orange juice for a while, as if hoping to discover the meaning of life in it, and then said, 'You know, *these* are the kind of people I am really interested in. Not that I want to *objectify* the poor, I don't mean to do that at all. I am very aware of all that. The real India, with their real stories, that smell of the earth itself. These people are so much in tune with their environment, so much closer to nature.'

Rani thought of the polythene bags that clogged the drains in their street, and how Bittu and his friends collected thin plastic bags just to blow them up with their mouths and burst them behind their schoolmasters.

'And the art of oral story-telling is just lost,' Dia continued. 'In fact,' she said, perking up, 'can I interview this girl Rani here for a documentary on oral story-telling that I am planning to make?'

Rani looked distressed at the thought of being interviewed. Sadhna saw the look on her face.

'We'll see. Maybe fix it up some day,' Sadhna said, trying to put Dia off.

After talking for about another half hour, Dia and Sasha finally left, leaving Sadhna exhausted and Rani bemused.

✧ ✧ ✧

Pradipto Ghosh was divorced. Rumours were rife that he was having an affair with Dia. He had a five-year-old son called Anuj and one day, he brought Anuj to visit Sadhna. Sadhna was a little surprised. They weren't special friends. But then Pradipto explained that his ex-wife was out of the country for a few days and he was having trouble keeping the boy occupied and happy.

'I thought a visit to some friends might do him good.'

Anuj had a small, heart-shaped face and wore glasses and a serious expression. When Rani saw him her heart filled with joy, and she wondered if Bittu's appearance had changed in the last few months since she had seen him.

Anuj was quiet. He did not smile much and refused any snacks or drinks offered to him. Something in his eyes tugged at Sadhna's heartstrings. She called Rani to her.

'Will you tell him a story, Rani?'

Rani looked shy and shook her head. But Sadhna drew her aside.

'The poor boy looks unhappy. Just tell him any story. Maybe he will cheer up.'

Rani sat down on the floor, looking vaguely into the distance again, trying to begin a story.

Pradipto and Anuj looked at her expectantly, and she began.

'Once, in the hot, dusty plains, was a beautiful village. Nobody was very rich in the village. But nobody was very poor either. There was a halwai with a big sweet shop who made jalebis and gulab jamuns every single day. All the children were naughty, uneducated and did at least one thing a day, if not more, that got them a slap from their mothers. In the evenings, they gathered around Nathu Ram Halwai. Those who had a fifty paise or so would buy a laddoo or a gulab jamun, and the rest would set up a clamour till either the others shared with them, or Nathu Ram, driven by rage, thrust large quantities of sweets into their hands just to get rid of them. However, since he had enough to eat himself, he never felt the lack of anything. The grown-ups weren't much better. Though most farmers worked hard, many idled. There was a man called Champat in the village who was a born story-teller. He would tell tales from the Ramayana, the Mahabharata and the Panchatantra. He was hardly well-versed with these stories. He knew the stories sketchily and filled up the gaps most imaginatively. In his versions of the stories, Draupadi went shopping when she got tired of her five husbands and haggled endlessly over brinjals and tomatoes. Ram's brother, Laxman, had lazy days during their exile in the forest and would lie under a tree all day, chewing grass stalks and not listening to a word that Ram or Sita said to him. The idlers would sit by Champat, listening to his endless stories. Some women would join in too, letting the rice burn in the kitchen while their children cried. The children would not cry for long, though, of course. They would head straight to Nathu Ram. It was an easy-going, laidback life. The lifestyles were deplorable; the men were not hard-working and stable enough. The women were not dutiful and the children had zero interest in learning.'

Here Rani halted, pleased with the village she had created.

Since Anuj was a little boy, she thought, if the tale was slightly moralistic, it might benefit him. It would be good for him to know that idleness and uselessness were no good in life, as she had often told Bittu with very little effect.

Rani continued:

'One day, two government officials in safari suits came to the village. They tsk-tsked at everything – at the ragged, barefoot, happy children; at the obese Nathu Ram; at the chattering women who washed clothes by the river, washing less and talking more; and at the idlers who grouped themselves around Champat, listening to another of his tall tales. They asked for the village headman. The headman was found lying on a charpai in his open courtyard, chewing betel leaves and staring at the clouds.

The government officials were thrown into despair. They were not of the usual corrupt variety. They took notes, interviewed people and then went to see the single-roomed building that was supposed to serve as a primary school. It was an airy and clean room. Women sat on the floor working at intricate embroidery, their babies and toddlers playing around them. The women seemed proud of this accomplishment. "These get sold in Delhi, at Janpath," they proudly said. Then the officials visited the single room that was supposed to be the village hospital. One part of the room was covered with crates and boxes of medical supplies while in the other part, the compounder lay on a chatai, his ears glued to a little transistor blaring out a cricket match commentary.

Horrified, the officials departed. The next two months brought a revolution to the village. The primary school was set up, children went there to study in uniform, their Nathu Ram dreams on hold at least till midday, and a nurse was stationed at the hospital with a first-aid kit. People were offered employment and the television cable connection was brought into the village. And so the village prospered. And the men and the women huffed and puffed to keep up with the changes.'

Rani ended, aware that this was not one of her best stories. Perhaps it was the alien audience that had affected her imagination. But now that she came to think of it, there was no story, no entertainment value. She had tried to convey that hard work was better than laziness. But it didn't seem to have worked. In the future, Rani thought, she'd steer clear of morals. She was no good at them. She looked up apprehensively, expecting to see disappointment on everyone's faces. Sadhna was looking at her in extreme pleasure. And Vina looked bored.

Anuj suddenly asked, 'But they did still get sweets from Nathu Ram's, right? At least sometimes?'

Rani felt a pang of remorse, 'Of course they did.'

Then she wildly added, 'And God appeared in Nathu Ram's dreams one night and instructed him to make small packets of mithai everyday without fail, and deliver one to every single child in the village.'

Anuj looked happy now. The story had a happy ending.

When Rani looked up at Pradipto, she was amazed. He was acting like a madman again. He leapt to his feet and said to Sadhna excitedly, 'Don't you see, don't you *see* what is happening here? In this story, this girl has turned everything upside down.'

Rani looked alarmed. What had she done *now*?

Pradipto started to pace the room. 'We are going to re-invent story-telling.'

Rani looked to Sadhna for comfort. Bittu had never reacted to her stories like this. Sadhna nodded at her reassuringly.

'Do you see what she has done?' Pradipto continued. 'She has turned everything around – all our notions, all our theories. A story of an unspoilt village – pastoral, idyllic, with innocent minds and children, with no preconceived notions, untainted by the education system, living happily as a community, and then,' Pradipto said, almost in agony, 'the State steps in with its schools, its textbooks, its rules and its morals.'

Pradipto had forgotten all about Anuj now. '*And*,' Pradipto added, 'not content with that, they bring the curse of television to the beautiful untainted village in the hills.'

'This village was in the hot, dusty plains,' Sadhna reminded him quietly.

'No matter,' Pradipto said, 'but they bring in television, turning this happy community into consumers, aspirants, dooming them to lives of unfulfilled desires. She has turned everything upside down.'

Rani looked decidedly guilty now.

'I have an idea,' Pradipto said, his spectacles kept carefully at a mad-genius angle. 'Let us have a book that combines your stories,' he said to Sadhna. 'Your stories are also about freedom from conditioning.'

'No,' Sadhna said. 'They are just normal stories I think of.'

Pradipto smiled indulgently. 'Two genius women in one household and neither knows it. This is big. This is *so* big. I am going to make it big. This girl, what is her name, Rani, we'll first have to translate her stories into English, and then put your best stories together. Maybe you can write a few new ones. And then we make a splash. The subaltern and the middle class finally meet. We will market it as the first of its kind in India, where social boundaries have finally dissolved and the tradition of story-telling has prevailed.'

'Take it easy, Pradipto,' Sadhna said, a little edgily.

But he continued, 'The publishing industry is tired. Intense young novelists, fantasy story writers, the diasporic experience, magic realism – every bloody thing has been done. This will be a breakthrough.'

Rani and Sadhna sat silent. Anuj was looking out the window.

'We can begin with a touching prologue about the sharing, caring relationship that you two share, about the love and understanding possible between two women from totally different classes! Breaking all barriers! And then a wide range of stories rich in local colour and emotion co-written by the two of you. Yes! Nobody can beat that,' he ended jubilantly.

Sadhna suddenly rose to her feet, disgusted. 'We are just being ourselves, Pradipto, just telling our own stories. What do you know of any love and understanding that we might or might not share? How do you know that we haven't fought like wild cats? It is not all about selling.'

Sadhna was also disgusted because by now she had conceived a deep affection and empathy for Rani. She felt profound resentment that the very world which had prevented Rani from being free of worries, financial and otherwise, and prevented her from cuddling up to Bittu to tell *him* her precious stories, should be so eager to market her 'subalterness', her freak value!

Rani just thought a person had to be really out of his mind to get so excited about the kind of silly stories she made up.

Pradipto looked taken aback at Sadhna's reaction. 'Well, think about it,' he said. 'It could mean a lot of money and exposure for you. And for the girl.'

'Her name is Rani,' Sadhna said coldly. And for the rest of Pradipto's visit, Sadhna proceeded to play with Anuj, teaching him how to make paper planes.

Rani, after years of Bittu's company, was an expert at paper boats and made a few. Even Vina chipped in, showing him how to make small paper balls that he could actually blow up with his mouth. They plied Anuj with French toast and banana milkshake. He had opened up to them now and asked for more ketchup with his toast. They helped him make patterns with ketchup all over his French toast and on the edges of his plate.

Anuj left happier. Pradipto left bemused.

Ten

The next morning, Rani was woken by a gentle spray of raindrops from the open window. It was another monsoon shower. She woke up happy and surprised – surprised because she had forgotten a bit about happiness. In Amritsar, too, her mattress had been by the window and when a spray of raindrops came in during the monsoon, she would make no effort to move away. She had always found that rainy days were happy days for her. Good things happened on rainy days. Bittu had always derided this as superstition but she clung to her belief.

Rani smiled and sat up in her bed. Vina was still asleep, her face white with the beauty cream that she coated on her face every night after removing her make-up. She had finally taken Rani's advice.

The trees looked fresher, greener. The porch of the house had a fibreglass cover. And the sound of the rainsdrops pattering onto it was magical.

After ages, the cold knot in Rani's heart seemed to loosen up a little, melt a little and happiness, though not flooding her heart, seemed to be tiptoeing in.

She also felt less lethargic, more energetic.

Rani sprang up, made her bed and went into the bathroom to take a long cold-water bath, washing her hair as well, pouring mug after mug of cold water on her head. The water fell on her scalp and made its way down her body, cooling her skin, moistening every pore, making a puddle around her toes. Rani began to hum,

Tujhe dekha to yeh jaana sanam,
Pyar hota hai deewana sanam ...

'Please, please shut up,' Vina shouted from her bed. She was not an early-morning person. Rani scrubbed herself raw with the bar of Medimix, rinsed it all off and stood for a while on the wet concrete floor, naked and peaceful, water still trickling from her hair.

Then she rubbed her body with Ayur moisturizer. She came out wrapped in a towel, picked out a yellow-and-white polka-dotted kameez, teamed it with a white salwar and chunni and rummaged in her luggage till she found her old wooden box. Rani discovered the crisp currency note that Dheeraj had given her on their last Dussehra. She kissed it and put it back. Then she took out a small bottle of moisturizer from the box and rubbed some her face. She also took out two yellow star-shaped earrings and put them on and ran downstairs, eager to begin the day's work.

Sadhna's eyes lit up at the sight of Rani. 'Somebody is all pretty today,' she said. 'Shahrukh Khan coming to visit?'

Rani blushed. 'Nothing like that,' she said.

'Didi,' she said urgently, 'please, please let me do your hair.'

'It's only seven in the morning. I have just taken a shower. At least give me my morning coffee first.'

'Just two minutes. Please.'

Sadhna acquiesced.

Rani was ruthless. She brushed and combed Sadhna's hair and tied it simply at the nape of her neck with a broad clasp. It was so simple yet suddenly made Sadhna look more elegant. Then she quickly cleaned Sadhna's face using cotton wool and a cleanser, followed it with moisturizing, added a touch of kajal, a hint of light pink lipstick and then declared herself satisfied. In her most professional manner, she handed a mirror to Sadhna.

Sadhna smiled.

'Yes, at least I don't look like something the cat has dragged in.' Secretly, Sadhna was touched.

'And now, can I have my coffee?'

Rani scuttled off to the kitchen.

She reappeared with the coffee in five minutes and said, 'Later, I will pluck your eyebrows.'

'Oh no, you won't,' Sadhna said. 'Now be quiet while I have my coffee.'

✧ ✧ ✧

Rani was in the kitchen, carefully polishing the taps. She thought of her days at home, happy hours whiled away with Seema, the bustle at Eve's Beauty Parlour, customers who came there vain, despairing or happy.

She thought of the precious figure swathed in white, now just ashes, each particle scattered god-knows-where.

She thought of Kavita, dead in her Anarkali kurta.

Of Vaishali and her briskness in matters of death and dinners. Of Sasha and her friends.

She thought of all the films she had seen, the news she had watched, the chatter of relatives and neighbours. These disjointed thoughts still did not add up to make any sense to her. However, Rani was learning that it was just not possible to make sense of everything.

She did not know why people talked to each other, made films, wrote stories, staged plays; what desperation led humankind to tell stories, to communicate? Were they seeking something inside those stories? She would never know and had lost the desire to know.

The taps shone.

She realized that the world was made up of stories, hers and other people's, real ones and imaginary ones. And that her father had died of exhaustion, trying to interpret these stories. But there was no point. They never could make sense. At least, not all of them. There were too many, they were too big. When Rani dwelled on them, she felt the same germ stir inside her, the germ that had been in Dheeraj. And it frightened Rani. For Rani, stories would never have sane, satisfactory endings.

All she knew was that while she was working at a parlour, even though she might be well aware that right then, at that very moment, millions of stories were being played out on this earth, her job was to just take out that one extra hair from an eyebrow, leaving a perfect shape behind.

✧ ✧ ✧

The monsoon was heavy that year. It rained every other day. All of Delhi groaned with traffic jams and waterlogged roads.

Then, one day, the call came. Vina answered it and called Rani. It was the chemist's wife. A parlour nearby, called Curls and Blushes, needed a trained girl urgently. She had recommended Rani and they wanted to interview her. 'But it is just a formality,' the chemist's wife said. 'I know they are really desperate. Two of their girls got married and left in the space of one month. And I spoke very highly of you. So mind you ask for a good salary.'

Rani could barely speak, but she managed to blurt out her thanks.

She rushed to Sadhna and Vina and told them. Both were happy, yet sad that she'd be leaving if she got the job.

'You know what,' Sadhna said thoughtfully, 'if you get this job, you can stay here till I am here. And later, you can find another room for yourself.' Rani smiled back at her, happy.

And that very evening, dressed neatly, Rani managed to locate Curls and Blushes.

It was a much swankier place than Eve's Beauty Parlour and Rani felt a momentary pang, as if she were betraying Asha.

A smartly dressed woman asked her some questions in a crisp voice, seemed satisfied with both the answers and with Rani, and asked her to demonstrate a few skills. Another girl who worked there was brought in as a guinea pig. She sat with great trepidation, relaxing as Rani gave her an efficient hair trim, threaded her eyebrows and made up her face.

Rani got the job.

'Isn't it wonderful?' Sadhna asked her warmly that evening. The two were getting closer each day.

'I suppose it is. But I do know one thing now. Anything can go wrong, any time,' Rani ended darkly, chopping the last carrot into tiny, neat pieces.

✧ ✧ ✧

It was pouring now. Water had begun to collect in the driveway and the trees looked as if they had just come back fresh from the laundry.

'Shall I make puris for breakfast today?' Rani asked.

Secretly delighted by Rani's cheer, Sadhna agreed, even though she did not much feel like having puris. 'Yes, yes, we can celebrate Rani's new job,' Vina said. Then, wistfully, 'I wish I had some fancy skills too.'

Rani and went into the kitchen and began the preparations. Vina joined her in ten minutes. She seemed to be in a joyous mood.

'Rain means no washing. That means no drying. And that means no ironing,' she said to Rani. 'I hope it rains for another week.' The two were in the middle of rolling out puris and planning the potatoes to serve with them when the doorbell rang.

'I'll answer it,' Vina offered.

She opened the door and peered at the gate. The postman, who rarely came by now except with bills, was standing at the gate, holding an umbrella over his head. 'Telegram,' he shouted.

Sadhna was intrigued. With e-mail and cellphones, one hardly ever saw or heard of a telegram.

It was for Rani, sent by Seema.

Mahesh had hung himself from the ceiling fan in his room.

He was dead.

✧ ✧ ✧

Sadhna and Rani stood looking at each other. Rani's hands were smeared with dough. She looked questioningly at Sadhna with a half-smile. Then she saw the pallor on Sadhna's face and the fluttering telegram in her hands. She was more familiar than Sadhna with the news of births, weddings, illnesses and deaths that telegrams carried. Her heart turned a tiny somersault. 'What is it, Didi?'

A wordless moment passed within them.

Sadhna handed the telegram to Rani with trembling hands.

When Rani tried to read it haltingly with doughy hands, Sadhna couldn't bear it and snatched the piece of paper back from her. They made eye contact and Rani gave her silent consent. Sadhna read out the cold, piercing words. The rain continued unabated.

Eleven

Rani packed in a dream.

Another auto.

More traffic. Another journey. The same crowds.

Rain lashed so fiercely now that it reached Rani, the water mingling with the tears on her face.

The train journey this time was even more terrible than Rani could ever have imagined. The words in the telegram resounded in her ears, unreal at times, accusing at others.

They sent her into a dream-like trance. Her recent anger at Mahesh seemed to melt away. She remembered the games they had played together in their childhood, sitting under the neem tree, fashioning clay toys, pots and pans from the soil there. They had built little brick houses, they had fed street dogs and their litters, they had carefully divided kheer between them in equal measures, going still and mute when they heard their parents calling them in for lunch. Their mother had died when they were children, died trying to bring another life into the world, so they had little memory of her. And Rani pictured Mahesh on his wedding day, looking embarrassed.

And then, the silent, sullen Mahesh, his dreams thwarted, talking little to her, passing Satish Electricals some days with a bowed head, stopping only to call out a greeting to Satish.

It was still pouring when the train reached Amritsar. Oblivious to it, Rani walked out of the railway station and got a cycle rickshaw.

The rickshawala was drenched as well but agreed to take her. Rani sat trembling as the rickshaw wended its way through familiar roads and streets towards Rani's old home. Rani could see the drenched back of the rickshawala. Through his dripping-wet white kurta, she could see a mole. A mole on an alive body. Why, why, why couldn't Mahesh be alive too? Tears came streaming down her face.

Once again, there was wailing outside the house. Rani hauled down her small overnight bag from the rickshaw, soaked to the skin. She paid the rickshawala without her usual bargaining and ran into the gate. People in white were huddled together in the verandah, sheltering from the rain.

She knew the cremation would be over by now; she would only be able to attend the prayer ceremonies. Numbly, Rani walked to the front door. Suddenly, she found a gaunt-faced Neelam blocking her way. Tears flooded Rani afresh as she saw the familiar face and felt the shared grief.

She was about to step forward when Neelam said, quietly, 'You can't come in.'

Rani thought she had misheard. She looked around at the other people but nobody would meet her eyes.

'Bhabhi,' Rani said through her tears. But Neelam remained stony. There were streaks of tears on her grief-ravaged face. Her hair was dishevelled and she looked almost demented. 'I won't let you step in,' she said, rage in every syllable. Rani stood there in the rain. She couldn't think clearly through her grief and confusion.

'Bittu,' Rani called desperately, longing to clasp him to herself.

Neelam almost snarled, 'You and your father and that wretched employer of Mahesh's, Charan Das, have together killed my husband. Don't you dare come near my son now! He is the one who found his father's body. He hasn't spoken a word or shed a tear since.'

Rani was stunned. Little Bittu had seen that? Her heart bursting with sorrow and hurt, Rani stood in the courtyard of her familiar home, the beautiful neem leaves dripping and Mahesh's cycle still in place.

The light overnight bag felt heavy, the rain washed over her and she stood still as a statue.

✧ ✧ ✧

Half an hour later, she sat numbly in Seema's room. Seema had come forward, quietly crying herself, had held Rani's hand and led her to her own home. She had ignored the look of disapproval on her family's faces.

Rani sat huddled in dry clothes on Seema's bed, unable to take a single sip of the tea that Seema had thrust upon her. Seema let her cry till she was drained.

Both girls were quiet for a few minutes.

Then Rani asked her, 'What is all this? Why? Why did he do it?'

'He left a note that doesn't say much. But a day before he ... he ... did it he had gone to visit Satish. He had poured out his heart to him. His employer, Charan Das, underpaid him and humiliated him whenever he got the chance. He hated his job but money was scarce. Neelam still nagged all day. And he felt guilty.'

'Guilty? What for?'

Seema looked away. 'He felt partially responsible for your father's death and for driving you away. He felt he had failed as a son and as a brother. And that he couldn't do the work he wanted to. He felt his life was futile.'

'Despite Bittu?' Rani asked, her heart breaking at the thought of the little boy gazing up at his father's body.

'Everyone is very worried about Bittu. Won't cry, won't talk. Poor little boy.'

After this, they cried again. The whole conversation was punctuated with fits of crying.

'He shared his problems with Satish but gave him no inkling of what he was planning to do. Just asked him to keep it to himself.'

'Then how do you know?'

'Everbody knows. Rani, Satish ... Satish got married.'

Rani waited impatiently. Satish seemed insignificant now.

Emboldened, Seema continued, 'Her name is Neetu. She looks

very benign but according to Bittu, when she is haggling for vegetables, she looks like a plump tigress in a sari.'

Rani gave a wan smile.

'Well, Satish told her and she is such an incorrigible gossip that within hours, the whole neighbourhood knew.'

Rani considered locating this Neetu and beating her brains in but it wouldn't help.

✧ ✧ ✧

Rani waited two days, going to and from Seema's house, begging to be let in to pray, begging to meet Bittu but Neelam was adamant and her brothers were effective sentries. At the end of two days, when Seema's family started making barbed comments about people who never brought peace with them, Rani had to leave. Without a glimpse of Bittu. She felt she could never be happy again.

She took the morning train. Seema, openly defying her family and even calling Rakesh a despot, went to the railway station to see Rani off. They hugged tight, knowing they might not see each other again, and Rani boarded another train for another journey where her demons would follow her. Rani also knew that she was leaving a precious part of her behind. Perhaps forever.

When the train moved out of the station, she saw beggars and vagrants on the platform. Rani's family had not been poor, not in this sense. It was amazing how a few rupees more or a few rupees less and the temperaments of individuals could, in a year, turn a fairly happy family into a nightmarish ruin. And then, from Amritsar to Ludhiana, she cried non-stop. What must Bittu be going through? The rest of the journey was spent in going to the stinking toilet and throwing up, till her stomach was empty and all she could produce was yellow bile.

Life was over, as far as she knew. She was no longer the Rani she had once been – she no longer knew her, liked her, disliked her or cared for her.

Yes, life was over.

✧ ✧ ✧

All Rani told Sadhna was that Bittu wouldn't cry or talk. Sadhna left her alone, did not probe much and warned Vina not to do so either, and yet made sure Rani was always occupied. All Sadhna said to Rani was, 'Maybe you'll go back one day. You will be able to meet Bittu. Your bhabhi will come around. Just give it time.'

When Pradipto, Dia, Nina, Sasha or any of their friends visited, Rani was just courteous to them; she wouldn't speak a word. Though Rani didn't understand these people, sheer instinct made her wary of them now. She couldn't put it into words, even to herself. She had nothing to say to them. They were fluff to her.

Initially they were a little offended, but there wasn't much they could do. The projects and plans Pradipto had with Rani in mind had to go, but he moved on pretty quickly.

Confusion could coexist with clarity.

✧ ✧ ✧

It was Rani's first day at Curls and Blushes. Sadhna and Vina had wished the stony-faced girl the best of luck and had received her half-hearted thanks.When she entered, she smelt the familiar smells of chemicals, make-up and shampoo. Hairdryers hummed and face steamers hissed. Here, the uniform was a pale pink apron with little red flowers on it. Rani put hers on and was called to thread a pair of eyebrows.

She went to the customer who looked up at her expectantly. Rani twisted the nylon thread around her fingers in a familiar motion. She had not realized what a part of her physical being that motion was. Then she bent and expertly, with a keen eye, turned the bushy, uneven eyebrows into beautiful, gentle arches that went superbly with the brown eyes underneath.

Acknowledgements

I would like to thank my family, friends and all the people in and outside publishing who helped bring this book into the world.